QUATERMAIN

THE NEW ADVENTURES

VOLUME FIVE

AIRSHIP 27 PRODUCTIONS

TM

Quatermain:The New Adventures Volume 5

Published by Airship 27 Productions
www.airship27.com
www.airship27hangar.com

Interior illustrations © 2019 Clayton Hinkle
Cover illustration © 2019 Ted Hammond

Editor: Ron Fortier
Associate Editor: Jonathan Sweet
Marketing and Promotions Manager: Michael Vance
Production and design by Rob Davis.

ISBN: 978-1-946183-73-6

Printed in the United States of America

10 9 8 7 6 5 4 3 2 1

QUATERMAIN

THE NEW ADVENTURES

VOLUME FIVE CONTENTS

Allan Quatermain vs The Royal Army

By
DeWayne Dowers

Its tremendous horns swayed rhythmically as it shook its head from side to side while it climbed out of the bog. Cool mud from the watering hole clung to its belly and legs as it snorted a warning call to its fellows. Hot air belched from its nostrils as it sensed something unfamiliar and dangerous nearby. The bull Cape buffalo seemed as large as a small elephant as he cleared the reeds and came into range of Allan Quatermain's rifle. Prey and predator paused for a moment and stood very still. The beast made eye contact with Quatermain right as he squeezed the trigger. Fire leaped from the long barrel and the single crackle from the rifle sent the remainder of the herd into a panic. Other shots rang out across the South African plain and more beasts fell ensuring that Quatermain's expedition would have food for the upcoming weeks.

"Fantastic shot old boy," cheered Daniel Perkins, a short, rotund statesman that was rather unremarkable other than being covered with red, bushy hair.

"It will keep us fed," responded Quatermain as he pulled a revolver from its holster before lifting himself from the ground.

"I'll say. Amazing. You didn't have to fire a second time."

Quatermain ignored Perkins. It irritated him that he had to kill. He no longer needed to hunt to make a living. He had more wealth than he could ever spend after his journey through the desert to King Solomon's mines. Hunting however was a necessity to feed his expedition.

"What's that gun for?" asked Perkins.

Before he could respond, a large cow reared to her feet and pushed toward the chunky politician. Quatermain lifted the English Bulldog and squeezed the trigger. The bark of the revolver caused Perkins to throw both hands in the air in an attempt to cover his head. He squealed in fright like a schoolgirl. The beast fell at the feet of Quatermain.

"Never underestimate this savage country. You are no longer in the House of Commons sir."

"Evidently." Perkins turned about and headed in the opposite direction of their camp.

"Perkins," grunted Quatermain "you are heading the wrong direction."

※ ※ ※

Several weeks prior, Allan Quatermain sat in his study waiting for an old friend. Seated with him around the hearth was Sir Henry Curtis and Captain John Good, RN. Curtis was a very large man and there was not a chair in the home that was adequately suited to his enormous frame. The Zulu had called him Incubu which meant elephant. His grey eyes were offset by his long blonde locks and blonde beard. John Good was a stark contrast to the handsome Henry Curtis. Good was a short, stout, dark skinned man with black eyes. Good was a meticulous dresser and wore a monocle over one eye.

"This will most likely be our greatest challenge," puffed Quatermain as he exhaled bellows of smoke from his pipe.

"Indeed it will be," offered Curtis.

John Good shook his head and said, "It's not as bad as all of that."

"It could be worse," laughed the aged hunter.

"This is a terrible plight that you have brought upon the mighty warrior, the slaughterer, the wielder of Inkosi-kaas, the friend of Macumazahn, the Zulu Chieftain, Umslopogaas," roared the displeased Zulu warrior.

"You look excellent," offered Good.

Umslopogaas refused to acknowledge the statement by John Good but eyed Allan Quatermain without blinking. The Zulu warrior wore a white ruffled shirt with a burgundy ascot. A vest was buttoned about his waist and a long burgundy coat hung from his impressive figure perfectly.

"Where are your pants, good fellow?" asked Good. The three men simultaneously glanced down and noticed that Umslopogaas stood in front of them with bare feet and wearing the traditional animal hide apron of his people.

His eyes still fixed upon Quatermain he said, "If you were not the mighty Macumazahn, I would split you in half with the broad end of Inkosi-kaas!" He then tore the ascot from about his neck and ripped the ruffled shirt from his body throwing it at the feet of his friends.

"I told you that this would be a challenge."

"Well, the jacket looks superb," mentioned Good. Umslopogaas smiled a toothy grin at the sea captain.

A few hours later a loud knock upon the vestibule door signaled the arrival of their expected guest. Umslopogaas sat on floor of the den in traditional Zulu fashion sharpening his axe as Allan Quatermain swung open the door and greeted Daniel Perkins who was accompanied by Admiral William Shone and Benjamin Bristol, a lieutenant in the Royal Army.

"Gentlemen," uttered Quatermain.

"It is good to see you again, Admiral," volunteered John Good.

"I'm grateful for the invitation," responded the Admiral.

They stepped through the vestibule and into the living area. It was then they noticed the imposing figure of Umslopogaas seated just a few feet away. The Zulu chieftain never looked up from his task but continued to sharpen his already razor sharp axe.

"You could have warned us that you had a savage as a guest," barked Lieutenant Bristol. He reached for his revolver but the Admiral seized his forearm.

"We are guests as well," said Shone. "My apologies. I hope that we have not offended you Mr. Quatermain."

"I wasn't the one that was called a savage."

"Umslopogaas, the slaughterer, the wielder of Inkosi-kaas, the Great Chieftain of the Zulu nation cannot be offended by these pink, puffy men."

Umslopogaas leaped to his feet whirling his axe overhead in a wide arc and allowed it to come to rest by his side. Lieutenant Bristol shoved Daniel Perkins behind him as he drew his pistol from its holster. But before he could squeeze trigger or even level it at the Zulu Chieftain, he found the rounded spike of Inkosi-kaas pressed against his throat. Bristol wisely lowered his weapon and returned it to its holster.

"This was truly a brilliant idea," whispered Sir Henry Curtis to the sea captain.

"Agreed," chuckled Good.

Later that evening after the tension subsided, Umslopogaas had retired to a small grove of yew trees that separated Quatermain's estate from the church where his son was laid to rest. It was a beautiful thicket and being amongst the low hanging branches and green fir eased the Zulu chieftain's bloodlust.

"Without the insistence of John Good, I'd never have agreed to receive you. I have no mind for soldiering," grumbled Allan Quatermain. "Nor for politics," he added staring directly at Daniel Perkins.

"I mentioned to our host that there was a matter of great import that you wished to discuss with him," explained Good.

"We need an expedition to carry Mr. Perkins into the interior of Africa and assist him in searching out Dr. David Livingstone. We have not received any correspondence from Dr. Livingstone and it is rumored that a man from New York has set out to find him. A man by the name of Stanley."

"If this Stanley has already taken an expedition to search for Dr. Livingstone, then what purpose would I serve?"

"We would like you to reach Livingstone before Stanley," remarked Daniel Perkins.

"Livingstone has made important medical discoveries," added Admiral Shone.

Quatermain did not respond. He hated the machinations of men.

"Livingstone is essential to the region. He has created a great deal of goodwill amongst the savages and opened up trade routes that would have never been possible without him," offered John Good.

"I had hoped to spare you all of the political ramblings," interrupted Admiral Shone.

"You had hoped to lie to me. I am certain that I still haven't heard all of the matter but I have heard enough,"

"If we do not find Dr. Livingstone, lives both British and native will be lost in great number," offered Sir Henry Curtis.

Quatermain settled into the plush, button back chair and stared at Benjamin Bristol. He was a bit of an enigma. He was only of average height and weight but maintained a fierce appearance. His back was straight and his jaw jutted forward with a cleft chin. A dark mustache clung to his lip and his eyes were a golden brown. He was much too old to be a lieutenant and there were hints of scarring that peeked from under his uniform. A revolver hung holstered on his right side and an enormous knife was sheathed behind it. Umslopogaas had held his axe against Bristol's throat but it was not out of fear that he had holstered his weapon. Bristol had been hardened by war.

Late that night, Quatermain awoke from a deep sleep with a start. He sat up in bed and looked out of a window toward the grove of yew trees where Umslopogaas had bedded down for the night. The Zulu warrior since arriving in England had refused to sleep indoors and found much comfort in the grove. Quatermain's heart was pounding in his chest and the palms of his hands were sweaty. The disturbing images had forced his eyes open and he considered it God's mercy. In his dream, the Zulu chieftain held his axe high overhead and was bringing the broad end of the blade to bear on Quatermain. The hunter raised his Webley revolver and squeezed the trigger. He watched the .450 bullet blaze from the short barrel and rip through Umslopogaas' throat. Blood poured down his neck covering his chest in crimson as the Zulu chieftain fell to his knees. Quatermain squeezed the trigger once more this time shooting Umslopogaas in the head.

❁ ❁ ❁

Two weeks passed since the night Quatermain killed the young lioness. He hoped it was nothing more than an odd occurrence provoked by hunger and the smell of blood, but as it turned out, the pride of lions were following the expedition. Every evening there were more incursions by the pride. It appeared the predators were searching for weak spots in the expedition's defenses. These attacks cost the lives of porters and oxen, not to mention a large amount of rations.

"What are you doing about the lions?"

"Mr. Perkins, you did realize there were lions in Africa before you set out on this expedition?" asked Quatermain with a blank expression.

John Good and Sir Henry Curtis chuckled at the sardonic manner in which Quatermain had answered the sweaty, little politician from the House of Commons. Umslopogaas smiled in a broad manner which somehow seemed to make the Zulu chieftain even more foreboding.

"They attack the camp every night. We were told that you were a hunter and a guide. You have led us straight to our deaths!"

"Umslopogaas thinks that your presence offends the gods and the demons and it is they who send the lions to devour the pink, puffy man with his awful red hair." Then unexpectedly, Umslopogaas threw both hands in the air and roared like a lion at Perkins. It frightened Perkins so severely that he fell backwards onto the ground from his seat and he was kicking with his feet trying to get away from the Zulu warrior. The hilarity of the moment was cut short however as two porters passed where they were seated carrying a large lioness. Lieutenant Bristol followed behind the porters carrying a spear with a thick haft that was over six feet in length. Perkins gained his feet and all those that were sitting there having their evening meal just stared as Bristol walked past. Perkins dusted himself off and followed the Lieutenant.

"One less to worry about," offered John Good.

"Who is this Lieutenant Bristol?" asked Sir Henry Curtis.

"He is a white demon. Inkosi-kass would poke a fine hole in this demon," blurted out Umslopogaas.

Quatermain did not offer an opinion of the man but merely watched as he walked by with the lion that he had killed with a spear. Then, he returned his attention to the bowl of broth and the dried Cape buffalo which were the makings of his dinner. It shouldn't have mattered how the lion had met his fate but it did and it was disturbing to Quatermain. He witnessed the Maasai and the Zulu hunt lions before with spears but only in groups. Many times a tribesman would die in attempt. He had never seen a white man kill a lion in such manner. It appeared Lieutenant Bristol was more familiar with Africa than he had initially led everyone to believe.

"Umslopogaas, take Sir Henry Curtis with you and make a wide sweep of the area. I want to know where the lions are laying during the day."

"Yes, Macumazahn."

"They will be about tonight," said Quatermain "be careful." Quatermain pulled his Webley revolver from its holster ensuring that it was loaded. "Good, accompany me to speak with the Lieutenant."

"Of course," responded Captain John Good.

※ ※ ※

Sir Henry Curtis was doubled over at the waist with his hands resting upon his knees in an attempt to catch his breath. He sucked down the warm evening air in great gulps as Umslopogaas stood nearby sneering at him. The Zulu chieftain glistened under the low hanging moon as sweat gathered upon his obsidian skin outlining every battle hardened muscle and contour of his body. He was deadlier than any adder and swifter than the eagle approaching its prey.

"Hippopotami cannot out run the leopard no matter how large his tusk," offered Umslopogaas.

Curtis did not respond but struggled to keep his dinner of dried Cape buffalo down.

"You stay here and rest. Umslopogaas will pursue the devils."

"Just a moment longer," huffed Curtis but Sir Henry Curtis was speaking to himself. The Zulu chieftain had disappeared. Curtis slowly raised himself up bringing his Winchester repeater to his shoulder as the moon vanished behind a string of clouds and the night suddenly became very dark. It seemed as if someone had drawn a heavy set of curtains across the sky blotting out even the smallest glimmer of light.

"Umslopogaas," whispered Curtis but there was no response only the uncomfortable stillness of the night. The fiery-necked night jars even fell silent and abandoned their raucous song. Sir Henry Curtis reached into his pocket and pulled out a match. He cradled his rifle under his arm and struck the match cupping it with his hand. He had wanted to light his pipe but in the warm glow of the match, he saw several pairs of eyes staring back at him. Slowly one by one the lions stepped out of the bush and stalked toward him. Curtis raised his rifle and took aim at a large female that circled to his right but at the sight of the rifle all of the lions began to growl. He considered squeezing the trigger but by this time eight or nine lions had broken through the underbrush and were approaching him with their mouths open revealing their horrible fangs. Sir Henry Curtis lowered his rifle and then the most peculiar thing happened. All of the lions simultaneously bolted past him and ducked into the dense brush directly behind him.

❀ ❀ ❀

Quatermain sat in an animal hide chair across from John Good in the tent of Lieutenant Bristol. The chairs were of ingenious design having ebony cross members wrapped in tanned elephant hide while the back of the chair was the plush skin of a large cat. It was most likely the hide of a jaguar but it was difficult for Quatermain to determine.

"Are you hungry?" asked Bristol "I can have my retainer, Lembui, prepare something."

"No need. We had just finished dinner when you returned from your hunt," responded Quatermain.

"It wasn't much of a hunt. I was merely scouting the outlying area and the beast charged me."

"Really? Do you always carry such a hefty spear with you when you are scouting?"

"It's not actually a spear. It's called a naginata. I had a blacksmith forge one to my specifications while I was in Japan. It's a fierce piece of work."

"Evidently."

"What is it that you have come to discuss?" asked Bristol.

Bristol pulled his soiled undershirt over his head revealing an innumerable collection of scars on his back. His chest and arms were covered in similar fashion. All of the scars were old wounds many of which were covered with proud flesh.

"I had hoped to speak with you and Daniel Perkins at the same time."

"Perkins is most likely hiding in his tent fearing another attack."

"Most likely," responded Quatermain.

"I can speak with Perkins later."

"We need to continue our course to the Zambezi River and from there we can follow it to the Great Lake," expressed Quatermain.

"Traveling along the Zambezi will not be an easy task with wagons and oxen," mentioned Bristol as he pulled a clean undershirt over his head and tucked it into his pants. He strapped on his holster containing a 1870 Glasser revolver.

"We might not have to worry with the oxen for much longer," laughed Good.

Quatermain stood to his feet studying Bristol for a long moment before saying anything. It was evident that Bristol had been in Africa for much longer than he wanted Quatermain to know. He surmised that the locked crates most likely carried weapons or ivory or both. He also realized that Bristol wasn't at all disturbed by the pride of lions that seemed to be hunting them.

"We will break camp in two days," instructed Quatermain.

"Why are we resting now?" asked Bristol.

"Not resting. Hunting. You are welcome to join us."

Sir Henry Curtis stood motionless for a great while as the mysterious shroud of clouds vanished in the wake of the marauding loins. The South African plain was illuminated by the low hanging moon once more and eerie shadows crawled along the ground. Quatermain asked him to search out the den of lions with Umslopogaas' help but the Zulu chieftain abandoned him. He couldn't help but surmise that a very dark magic was at work. It had caused the hunting party of lions to rush past him without attacking and had eclipsed the moon from sight.

"Umslopogaas, we have much to discuss when I see you again, old friend," muttered Curtis to himself. He estimated that he was at least three miles from the encampment and most likely the lions would be closing on the expedition momentarily. He lifted his rifle to his shoulder and fired a warning shot. He ejected the shell and fired another round.

"Umslopogaas," yelled out Curtis. There was no response.

White wispy tendrils spread across the sky cloaking the encampment in darkness while gaping mouths of the marauding lions tore at the unsuspecting oxen. They hadn't come to feed because their bellies were already full. They were driven by an unnatural lust for blood and they found it in ample supply at Quatermain's encampment. The oxen bellowed in agony alarming the entire expedition that the lions had returned.

Quatermain picked up his Winchester repeater and stepped out of his tent cautiously. He raised his rifle to his shoulder while peering down its open sights and squeezed off a shot that ripped through the hind quarter of a lion that had attacked a porter. The porter was tackled by the beast and was kicking at it trying to get away, but the lion gripped it tightly with its claws sinking his teeth into the man's thigh. The lion yowled in pain after the hefty round rendered its back legs useless but it continued to attack and shake the porter that it had caught between its jaws. Quatermain's next shot broke the beast's neck crumpling the animal on top the wounded porter.

"Help, someone help me," called a voice in the chaotic darkness. Quatermain immediately recognized the wheezing cry of Daniel Perkins. He held a seat in the House of Commons and was a skilled politician but he was ill suited for this type of campaign. Daniel Perkins was a short, plump, obstinate fellow. His head and arms were covered in bushy red hair which coupled with his dirty complexion and bumpy skin made the man less than attractive. He took his duties very seriously and was laborsome to endure in all matters. However, Quatermain did not want anyone to perish from being mauled by a lion.

"Perkins," yelled Quatermain.

"Over here, in my tent," responded Perkins.

A derringer barked illuminating a dark tent and Quatermain saw the silhouette of Perkins standing on top of a steamer trunk trying to escape one of the marauders. Perkins fired his derringer once more emptying its last barrel on the attacking lion. The beast growled and leaped for the odd little man as Quatermain made the entrance of the tent. A single shot to the back of the head left the lion dead at Daniel Perkins feet.

"Thank you," whined Perkins.

"Stay here. I have to find my men."

Perkins complied with Quatermain's demands and climbed inside of the steamer trunk shutting the lid tightly behind him.

"Good," called out Quatermain but there was no response. The pale cloud bank that had preceded the attack had now settled into the encampment like a thick fog. Fires burned here and there but the fog choked out any light making it impossible to see. Quatermain slung his rifle across his back and pulled his Webley revolver from its holster. A rifle was useless in these conditions.

"Good!" yelled Quatermain but again there was no response. The smell of blood, smoke, and fear filled the air. "Nothing more wretched than a damnable lion."

"Quatermain!" The voice was weak and shaky but distinguishable. It was the voice of Captain John Good.

"Good?" asked Quatermain as he whirled about in a circle trying to ascertain his location in the thick fog and now billows of smoke.

Stumbling toward him was a bloodied and bruised officer of her Majesty's royal navy. The fingers of his right hand were wrapped around the haft of his saber in a white-knuckle grip while his left hand was pressed against his throat. Thick, black blood seeped through his fingers from a nasty claw mark on his neck. His khaki shirt and trousers were shredded and soiled from the battle with the marauding lions.

"There's more than fifteen of these vile creatures," grunted Good but he was cut short by the bellow of Quatermain's revolver. Lead and fire leaped from the bulky revolver rendering the attacking beast lifeless just a few feet to the rear of Good.

"Fourteen then," shuddered Good.

"Fourteen," agreed Quatermain.

"We need to make it to the ridge and free ourselves from this fog."

"It's not fog."

"What is it then?" asked Good.

"Strong medicine." Quatermain pulled the trigger on his revolver and struck an advancing lion high in the shoulder. The heavy round struck bone with a sickening 'thud' but the sizeable beast reared up on its hind legs and tackled Quatermain to the ground. Its wide mouth stretched itself around the neck of the hunter but before it could close Good drove his saber through its throat. The beast turned its head mewling after its attacker but collapsed a moment later on top of Quatermain.

"Strong medicine indeed," gasped Good as he pulled his sword from the throat of the lion.

"Get this thing off of me," offered Quatermain.

It took great effort for the two injured compatriots to finally roll the lioness from off of the hunter. Good lifted Quatermain to his feet and they continued making their way toward the ridge while the screams of

"There's more than fifteen of these vile creatures."

dying men and women echoed through dark night. Blood, smoke, and mud mingled into a reeking froth that clogged the nostrils and turned one's stomach on end. It was the most awful night that Quatermain had spent in this savage land.

"Even the best of men could die on a night like tonight," growled Quatermain.

The hunter had barely finished speaking when two awful yellow eyes appeared in the midst of the pale clouds. A nose that was black as charcoal and moist with the night air broke through the haze next. It was the size of a dinner plate and puffed what appeared to be steaming billows from its nostrils.

"What is it?" whispered Good in hopes of not angering the creature.

Before the hunter could respond, the entirety of its white face pushed through the chalky cloud revealing it's beautiful yet terrible mane. "It's a white lion," said Good.

✺ ✺ ✺

"Blimey, god of the underworld!" yelped Sir Henry Curtis as he stared into the amber eyes of twenty-five blood drenched jackals. Their yellow teeth were clinched together as they growled expressing their consummate displeasure in having their evening meal interrupted.

The jackals intelligently formed a wedge like attack that collapsed into a circle about Sir Henry Curtis as the center held and the vile creatures flanked him on both sides.

"Bloody hell, this isn't going to end well, Ole boy." Curtis mumbled to himself as he lifted his Winchester repeater. It was at that instant that Curtis heard a horrible but familiar cry and Umslopogaas leaped over the rabid beast landing next to him with Inkosi-kass whirling about overhead.

"The mighty Incubu is trapped by the mangawana," laughed Umslopogaas.

"Not that I'm not thrilled to see you but it appears that the Woodpecker is trapped now," responded Curtis referring to the dreadful Zulu chieftain.

"The Woodpecker is not trapped as long as he holds Inkosi-kass. The slaughterer will bathe in the blood of these creatures like he has the mighty lion, the unstoppable hippopotami, and the stealthy jaguar. These jackals will line my bed tonight in soft fur." And with that, Umslopogaas swung Inkosi-kaas about in a wide arc and brought it crashing down splitting the skull of an encroaching dog in half.

"Strong medicine," groaned Umslopogaas as he watched the jackals refuse to die.

"Zulu medicine men?" asked Curtis as he fired his rifle again.

"Bah," spat the angry savage. "I have never seen such demons before."

A golden speckled jackal crawled across the ground clacking its teeth together in an attempt to bite Curtis. Its hind legs were limp and useless because one of Incubu's errant shots only wounded it and did not kill it. Curtis and Umslopogaas stepped back in wonderment at the furious beast as it continually tried to attack them even though its back was broken and its life's blood was pouring out onto the ground.

"Even in death it continues to attack," gasped Umslopogaas "It could be Zulu." The chieftain whipped his gruesome axe about his head and brought it down violently onto the jackal severing its head from its body.

In unison, the remnant of the pack lunged forward latching themselves unto Incubu and Umslopogaas with their jaws and began shaking them violently. Curtis swung his rifle like a club knocking a few of the beast off of Umslopogaas but both Curtis and Umslopogaas were wounded sorely in the attack. The Zulu fell to the ground under the weight of the barrage with the jackals tearing at his arms and legs. It was only Curtis' great strength and massive frame that allowed him to stay upright. Curtis dropped his rifle and began to peel the jackals from his body one by one snapping their necks between his massive fingers and hands as he tossed them aside. Soaked in sweat and thick, sticky blood, Incubu dropped to one knee weakened and dizzy with his head resting in both hands. He knew he should help his Zulu friend but found himself unable to move. The warm earth smacked Curtis in the face as the English gentleman fell prostrate to the ground. His sweat mingled with the dew as he slipped into unconsciousness.

The white lion stood in front of Quatermain with its head held high as it stamped its front paws against the ground. Its nearly transparent mane sparkled against the dark African night as light seemed to gather and refract about the terrible beast. Quatermain noticed it long before Good but it was Good who ultimately mentioned the clouds had lifted when the monstrous lion had appeared. It seemed the enormous white lion had orchestrated the attacks and even the fog obeyed its commands.

"Shoot the damn thing," shouted Good.

Quatermain ignored Good and stood his ground marveling at the animal. It stood an easy six foot tall at the withers and must have been over eight feet in length. Its hide was not stained nor off-color but it was the purest of whites making the beast even more dreadful. Quatermain studied it carefully without moving, barely allowing himself to breathe.

"Shoot it!" yelled Good.

Good dropped his saber and pulled his revolver from its holster pointing it at the blanched beast. He pulled the hammer back slowly and lined up its sights just below the jaw line of the lion. The animal twisted its head looking at Good as if it had never seen a man before much less a gun. The naval captain hesitated a moment longer then finally squeezed the trigger on the cumbersome revolver.

"Put the gun away, you damn fool," growled Quatermain, but before he could finish speaking, the miscreation sprang forward with a horrible ferocity knocking both the old hunter and Good to the ground. The awfulness of the blow left both of the explorers disoriented and scrambling to get away from the rending claws of the lion.

"Maybe shooting it wasn't the best of ideas," admitted Good as he crawled on all fours trying to escape with his life.

"You might as well have tugged on its mane," grumbled Quatermain as he rolled onto his back and pulled his revolver free from its holster but before he could pull back the hammer on his gun, the beast swiped it from his hand.

Quatermain stared into the yellow eyes of the ghastly beast and it occurred to him they looked vaguely familiar and particularly human. A grin spread across the animal's face revealing blood stained, pointed teeth as it lowered its snout sniffing Macumazahn. The lion nudged the hunter with his nose as if he was checking to see if Quatermain was still alive. It would have been a horrifying experience with a normal sized lion but this animal's nudge carried the force of a sledge hammer and Macumazahn let out a grunt.

"I never thought it would have been lions," mentioned Good faintly.

"What would have been lions?" asked Quatermain.

"Our demise. I never thought it would have been at the hands of a lion."

"I'm not dead yet."

The large white lion swung its enormous head about and started to saunter off back toward the ridge but not before grabbing Macumazahn by the ankle dragging the hunter along with him. Quatermain yowled in pain and writhed about trying to free himself from the jaws of the lion.

Macumazahn pounded against the lion's ribs with both fists but it proved to be of little distraction to the animal.

"I'm on my way ole boy," yelled Good as he scooped up Quatermain's revolver along with his own. The hunter was in no place to discuss a proper plan of action so he just continued to smash his fist into the side of the animal. He hoped against hope that Good would not shoot him in the attempt to rescue him.

Good squeezed off a shot with his revolver as he ran after the white lion and Macumazahn. He fired a second shot being careful not to hit Quatermain. The lion did not break his stride but continued toward the ridge. A third shot hit the lion in the hind quarter causing the beast to cry out in pain and bound forward still dragging the hunter along with him. Good fired twice more and both shots hit their target.

"Die, you filthy beast," screamed Good as he aimed his revolver at the base of the white lion's skull. He released the breath from his chest and gently squeezed the trigger. Good could not afford to miss if he wanted to see Macumazahn alive again. It was only a fraction of a second before the hammer would have fallen but Good saw something stir in his peripheral vision and he swung about to greet a charging lioness. He pulled the trigger on the revolver as the beast leaped toward him with her claws outstretched. It was an excellent shot and the bullet split the lion's skull in half. The naval officer was knocked backwards from the force of the attack and the lioness fell on top of Good.

"Dang, good shot ole boy! Dang good shot!" exclaimed Good congratulating himself but as he rolled the lion off him his heart sank. Good saw the white lion climb over the top of the ridge dragging Quatermain with him.

"God help us all," whispered Good.

Quatermain opened his eyes slowly considering whether or not he might be awakening in a very different place than the savage country that he once loved. He had been taught since he was a child about a place where the worm doesn't die and the fire is never quenched. He was quite relieved that the heat was bearable and there were no evident flames. He tried to lift his head and get to one elbow but the effort was too great. The old hunter collapsed resigned to his fate that he would die in Africa and not England. He closed his eyes and exhaled all of his breath. It was fitting that he would die in Africa and at the paws of a mighty beast. As he contemplated seeing his son once more, he heard a motion behind him but was in too much agony to move. He laid very still in hopes that whatever it was might not have noticed that he was still alive.

"You will not die this day, Allan Quatermain."

"Who are you?" asked the hunter wearily.

"I am whom you have hunted and killed. I am he whom you have trod upon and slept with. I am the one that you abandoned and then returned to," spoke a deep resounding voice that echoed within his head like a great flood of waters. "I am your only love."

"My only love died many years ago and I buried her. I haven't hunted you," whispered Quatermain in an almost inaudible voice because he knew that he was losing his mind. He knew it had to be his great thirst or the incredulous headache that he suffered from. He was going mad.

"Rest Allan Quatermain. Rest now."

Captain John Good of the Queen's Royal Navy had left Lieutenant Bristol on the ridge. He had assigned certain character traits to Lieutenant Bristol based on the fact that he was an officer in service to the Queen. He felt that Bristol was a man of honor and a man that could be trusted. Good had seen the scars that marked Bristol's body like medals of honor and knew that he was a fighting man. All of that changed on that ridge.

"Perkins, where have you been?" barked Good.

"I was told by Quatermain to remain in my tent. So I did," grunted Perkins. He was also freshly bathed and wearing a starched set of clothing.

"This is no place for politicians," Good growled at Perkins. He wanted nothing more than to pull his head from his shoulders. He resented the fact that Perkins had hid in his tent and all of his friends were destroyed by the lions.

"I am inclined to agree with you, Captain."

"Shut your mouth. You need to figure out how many oxen survived. You need to get a count on the porters and other servants. I also need to know how we are fixed on rations. Surely, you can handle that," chided Captain John Good.

Perkins nodded and didn't respond. Captain John Good hobbled through the encampment leaning heavily upon his crutch. He nudged at the scorched ground with his foot. He turned over the blackened pages of a book that had blown free from one of the tents. Only Bristol's tent and Perkin's stood intact.

"You should rest that leg. You are really of no use to us injured," remarked Bristol as he walked past Good. "We are breaking camp in the morning and moving north toward the Zambezi River."

"What about the rest of our party? Quatermain. Curtis. Umslopogaas."

"Quatermain and Curtis are most likely dead and as far as that Zulu goes," spat out Bristol "He most likely has something to do with this."

Good reached down instinctively for his revolver but it wasn't there. Bristol smiled and strode over to where Good was standing. He pulled the large revolver from his belt and pointed it at Good.

"Looking for this?" asked Bristol. He paused for a moment studying Good but the naval officer didn't respond. Bristol laughed and stepped closer to Good. He slipped the revolver into the holster on Good's belt. "Don't forget. We leave at first light."

Captain John Good pulled the revolver from its holster with remarkable speed and pointed it at the back of Bristol's head. Bristol stopped mid-stride when he heard the weighty hammer of the revolver cock into place. The Lieutenant slowly turned to face Good without uttering a word. Good locked eyes with Bristol as he slowly squeezed the trigger and hammer fell on an empty chamber making an awful screech.

"Hmmm," Good said "must be your lucky day, ole boy."

"We leave at first light," whispered Bristol through gritted teeth. Bristol regarded Good for a space time with his hand resting on the hilt of his knife that was fastened to his belt. He was unarmed other than the blade and Good was at least ten paces away. Good did not lower the revolver but aimed it coolly at Bristol's head. The Lieutenant lowered his gaze and spat upon the ground as he turned from the Captain and walked away.

"Fopdoodle," remarked Good as he watched Bristol walk away.

Quatermain shifted about on the cool, hard rock trying to get comfortable as he slept. He pulled the supple animal hide up to his neck and it was only the brush of its fur that awoke him with a start. He blinked several times trying to focus on his surroundings but his eyes were matted shut with sleep.

"Hello," he muttered as he tried to sit up. His muscles were stiff and unresponsive preventing him from rising. Quatermain touched his thigh that had been in the lion's mouth but all he could feel was a damp bandage and the intricate bindings that held it in place.

"Hello," he called out in a louder voice but still no one answered him. He ran his fingers over the bindings and the bandages. Quatermain knew that it was a skilled hand that had been attending to his wounds but he couldn't imagine who would have been able to rend him free from the clutches of the enormous white lion.

"Why didn't the lion kill me? Why am I still alive?" Quatermain spoke out. He stared upward at a large rock formation noticing that water trickled from the ceiling of the cave down the walls and then it drained backwards into the dark recess of the cavern. He turned his head about and stared into the darkness behind him thinking that he would rather be surrounded by a thousand Maasai warriors then to be lying in this cave injured and defenseless. His thoughts were interrupted when he heard a rustling at the mouth of the cave. He struggled to focus at what seemed like several men crawling into the cave through a small fissure some distance in front of him. He quickly realized that it wasn't men but the pride of marauding lions returning to their home. He lowered himself slowly to a prone position hoping not to draw attention to the fact that he was still alive. It was one thing to die alone in a cave but it was an entirely different matter to be torn to shreds by a pack of lions in that same cave. He unbuckled the clasp on the sheath that held his knife securely by his side and pulled it slowly free. Quatermain tried to quiet himself and calm his breathing. The first lioness approached with her head low against him. She nudged him with her nose and pawed gently at his arms. She nuzzled his neck with her large, wet nose and sniffed him. Then she lay down beside him resting her head across his chest. Quatermain's heart was pounding within his breast while his lungs felt as if they were set on fire. He could not control his breathing and he was sweating profusely. The second lioness arrived with no incident. She merely curled up next to him. Ten minutes passed as the marauding lions filed in one by one and laid down beside him. Finally, the large white lion squeezed himself through the fissure and lay down at the head of the cave. Quatermain thought to himself that he must be taken with a fever or that his thirst has driven him mad. He had seen it before when traveling the desert. He has seen men driven mad by the heat. Quatermain surmised that he had lost his mind and it wouldn't be long before he would see his son again. That thought was no small comfort in such desperate times.

Captain John Good was halting on one leg back toward the ridge when he saw a large, dark figure approaching dragging something behind him. He squinted through his spectacle and realized that it was Umslopogaas that was making his way toward the encampment. Good called for one of the porters and ordered that he assist the Zulu chieftain. Minutes later they had Sir Henry Curtis situated in Perkins tent on a bed of stretched water buffalo hide and other pelts.

"What happened to Curtis?"

"Umslopogaas was separated from Incubu when Macumazahn ordered us to search for the lions. He was attacked by the jackals," panted the Zulu chieftain.

"Jackals?" asked Good.

"Strong medicine. The jackal continued to attack even after being gravely wounded. The jackal stopped only after its head was severed from its body," grunted the weary Umslopogaas.

"We need to clean out those wounds," responded Good. He laid his crutch to the side and began to wash away the mud that Umslopogaas had covered him in.

"Stop. The mud draws out the fire," warned Umslopogaas.

"We need to attend to the bites to keep them from festering," argued Good.

"This is my home. My land. It is not the home of fat, pink men. Incubu fell to a dark curse. Demons attacked the mighty Elephant. It is only Macumazahn that can help Incubu now," growled Umslopogaas as he rose to his feet.

"Allan Quatermain is dead," responded Perkins as he stood to his feet as well.

Umslopogaas whipped Inkosi-kass upwards striking Perkins in the gut with a vicious blow that lifted him from the ground and landed him on his backside. The Slaughterer whirled the axe about overhead and would have split the politician in half had it not been for Good stepping between them.

"We don't know if he is dead," blurted out Good. "The white lion carried him off over the ridge and we haven't been able to find him."

"Umslopogaas would know if Macumazahn was dead," spat out the Zulu Chieftain.

Perkins retched up what little he had eaten for breakfast and afterwards laid there motionless where he had fallen hoping not to anger Umslopogaas further. The Zulu chieftain knelt placing his hand upon Incubu's chest muttering words so faintly that they could not be discerned. He touched his forehead to the forehead of Sir Henry Curtis. "I will make you better and then we together will find Macumazahn," he whispered to Curtis. He turned and looked at Perkins. "Get out. This is no longer your tent."

"Incubu will live. We will find Macumazahn. Then I will kill the Lieutenant and the politician for bringing these demons upon us," muttered Umslopogaas angrily.

"Bristol is leaving at first light heading north toward the Zambezi River," offered Good.

"The Lieutenant will die before the Woodpecker can take his life. The Zambezi River is filled with crocodile and hippopotami. He will never survive."

"Regardless, he leaves in the morning," responded Good as he settled in next to Curtis. "We need to rest."

That evening sleep visited all of them. It was a heavy, restful sleep brought on by more Zulu medicine. A flat rock had been set in the middle of the tent with several flowers from the Impepho plant laid carefully upon it with a small amount of dried grass for kindling. A fire was lit under the petals and the sweet odor of the plant filled the tent and rendered everyone unconscious. They awoke the next morning with Sir Henry Curtis standing over them naked and covered in the noxious brownish-green paste that Umslopogaas had prepared.

"Curtis for all of our sakes put on some clothes," yelped John Good as he awoke startled to see all of Incubu standing in front of hm.

"The mighty Incubu wears the armor of a true warrior," laughed Umslopogaas.

"You damn savage he's wearing nothing at all," groaned Good as he threw Curtis a pair of pants.

"Zulu warriors are born with armor. Skin black as night and hard like iron," exclaimed Umslopogaas.

Sir Henry Curtis stood blinking for a few moments uncertain of what had transpired over the last couple of days and ultimately decided that pants might be a good option. "Where is Quatermain?" he asked but before anyone could answer Umslopogaas let out a cry that was unlike anything heard before.

"Inkosi-kass has been stolen," hissed the Zulu chieftain.

✾ ✾ ✾

"Daniel in the lion's den," whispered Allan Quatermain. This is God's judgement he thought. "I have been cast into the lion's den just like that Hebrew boy." He laughed a sad, sobbing chuckle. He raised his hand slowly and touched the ruff of the neck on the lioness that rested her head on his chest. She pressed her head backwards against his hand encouraging him to give her a good scratching. Quatermain laughed loudly at this.

"I'm dead and this my hell. I'm trapped in a small, dank cavern with the most dreadful of all animals."

"You are not dead and you will not die in the jaws of these beasts," spoke that same ominous, resounding voice.

"Who are you?" howled Quatermain.

"I am Eshu."

"Eshu? You said I had loved you, that I had hunted you and killed you. You said that I had slept with you, abandoned you, and now returned to you."

"You have done all of these things."

"If I had killed you, then how are we speaking? If I loved you, how is it that I have had to ask your name?"

A small, frail boy stepped from the shadows weaving his way through the slumbering lions. He knelt beside Quatermain and stared at him with a scowl. The boy could not have been more than nine years old. His skin was dark as obsidian and it hung off of him like he hadn't been fed in weeks. He twisted his head about staring at Quatermain with his cold, gray eyes.

"Who are you?" asked Quatermain.

The boy reached out a single bony finger and touched the lips of Macumazahn. He then leaned over and examined Quatermain's bandages as his long blonde hair fell around his face hiding his expression. Suddenly, the wraith-like child clapped both hands together rubbing them vigorously against one another. He then placed his hands on Quatermain's hip and spoke strange but beautiful words over the old hunter. Heat leaped from the fingertips of the child spreading throughout the body Quatermain like

"Daniel in the lion's den."

fire upon parched ground. It licked at every nerve ending dancing its way from his hip, down his leg and out of his toes. Quatermain convulsed in agony arching his back and trying to speak but not words came from his mouth. The old hunter collapsed once more against the limestone floor.

"Rest Allan Quatermain. Rest now," said Eshu.

※ ※ ※

The journey toward the Zambezi River was an arduous one after the loss of many of the men and all but a few of the beast to the marauding lions. Bristol led the exhibition and Perkins trailed closely behind him on one of the remaining wagons. Sir Henry Curtis and Captain John Good followed at the rear of the caravan in the other wagon and had only agreed to travel forward at the urging of the strange child. They were still gravely concerned about the welfare of Quatermain and now that of Umslopogaas.

"This may very well be the last of our adventures," sighed Good.

"We have been in tighter spots than these before and made it through to the other side," answered Curtis.

"Aye, we have but we always had that damn savage at our side and Macumazahn at our backs. Now they are lost to us and we are following a viper whose only friend is a man that has the face of a ferret."

"Good, you worry like my old school marm. Nothing could ever satisfy her."

"Fate, chance, or just bad luck has dealt us some bitter blows as of late," offered Good. "It's no wonder I worry."

At that, nothing more was said between the two of them for a great while. They were content to ride in silence with Curtis manning the reins and Good keeping a watchful eye for any more surprises.

※ ※ ※

"He-who-sees-in-the-dark," whispered the shade of a boy with obsidian skin and blonde hair. "Watcher-by-night," he hissed in Quatermain's ear. "Macumazahn, it is time to awake from your slumber," groaned the child as he smote the old hunter in the side.

"What is it!" growled Quatermain only to see the dark, afflicted boy standing over him.

"You must regain your strength, Macumazahn."

Quatermain sat up slowly. He glanced toward the fissure where light ripped through rock and pushed back the darkness illuminating scant portions of the cavern. He saw only one lion lying with his paws crossed and his head raised at the entrance of the cave. He still was a predator and very deadly but just not as impressive as some of his kin. The lion arose to his feet when he noticed that Quatermain was awake and the beast began to move slowly toward the hunter. Quatermain realized immediately that the young lion had recently been in a fight with another more dominant lion. The left side of the lion's muzzle was bloody and the flesh was torn away by a heavy paw mark.

"If Macumazahn wishes to live, he must kill this beast and eat of its flesh," whispered the boy.

"I cannot kill this lion with my bare hands!"

The boy dropped the revolver that he had stolen from Good on the limestone floor. Macumazahn stared at it in amazement for a moment realizing that this was his Webley that he had dropped during the attack by the white lion. He scooped up the weapon checking to make sure that it was loaded and then shoved it into the face of the wraith like child.

"None of this is true. Either I have been taken by a fever and this is all just a dream or I have finally gone mad," exclaimed Quatermain.

"You may be taken with a fever and you have been mad with insanity for many years but this is no dream. If you do not kill that lion, he will gnaw on your bones for many days," cackled the boy.

Quatermain turned his head to ascertain the whereabouts of the lion noticing that beast was in no hurry to attack and then turned back to the odd little boy only to see that he had disappeared completely. A giggling, slight voice echoed from the recesses of the cavern behind Quatermain. The old hunter ignored the child and cursed the gods of this savage land under his breath. He stood up gingerly lifting the revolver and aiming it just below the slight mane of the young lion. The beast perceived that the revolver was a threat and bolted toward Quatermain. The beast covered a great deal of the cave with a single bound and would have been on top of the hunter with another stride but Macumazahn squeezed the trigger on the Webley revolver and flame belched from the barrel. Fur and blood flew as the hefty round tore through the young lion's shoulder crippling it. Quatermain fired a second shot hitting the beast in the chest crushing the animal's heart. The young lion sighed and crumpled to the ground as did Quatermain.

"Look at your quarry, Macumazahn," bellowed Eshu. "Look at what you have killed."

Quatermain had collapsed from exhaustion after firing the Webley revolver. He had fallen into a deep sleep for many hours. The opening of the cave was dark and the only light came from a small fire that burned in a crudely formed fire pit to his left. Bits of flesh roasted on a spit over the fire and a clay pot with whimsical symbols painted on its side appeared to be filled with milk and sat next to the fire. Quatermain lifted his head and eyed the young lion that he had killed. Except it wasn't a lion that he had shot. Laying in front of him was a beautiful, dark skinned woman with long black hair that was curled in ringlets. She wore a calfskin dress that left her shoulders bare and fell mid-thigh on her. Both wrists were adorned with circlets of gold and on each finger she wore a ring. The rings were either gold or silver alternatively and each held a precious stone at its center. Her beautiful golden eyes were fixed upon him but they were as lifeless as the limestone floor. Blood stained the ground where she had fallen.

"Why Macumazahn did you murder your lover?" asked Eshu.

"I shot a lion," muttered Quatermain "that was attacking me."

"Where is this lion?" roared the voice of Eshu from the depths of the cavern.

Quatermain turned to face the voice. His head was swimming with confusion and his surroundings seemed to twist about him. "I don't know."

"Look there at your quarry, Macumazahn."

Quatermain turned back to where the body of Umslopogaas laid. Inkosi-kass, with its rhinoceros horn handle and its beautiful inlays of gold, was broken in half and lying next to him. The Zulu chieftain stared at Macumazahn with lifeless eyes. Quatermain shook his head hoping to loosen the image from his mind but when he opened his eyes the Zulu was still dead on the cavern floor.

"Why Macumazahn did you murder your friend? A man that pledged his life to your service."

"I did not know that woman and I did not kill her. I did not murder Umslopogaas. This must all be a dream." Quatermain tried to rise to his feet but his legs were too weak to hold him. He fell to ground and curled into a ball with his arms wrapped about his head.

"This land that you have loved is dying and what has become of its people? What have you done to protect these that you love from the burglar? What have you done to save them from the murderer?" asked Eshu.

"Stop. Stop. Stop talking!" groaned Macumazahn.

❋ ❋ ❋

"Macumazahn, you need to eat." The blonde haired, dark skinned boy sat by the fire across from Quatermain in a cross legged position. "Allan Quatermain, you need to arise."

A faint glow from the evening sun trickled through the fissure making the cavern appear less ominous than before and gave it a sense of warmth and hominess. It was of little comfort however when Quatermain turned his face from the opening of the cave toward the fire where the child sat. If Eshu's voice had been unsettling, the voice of the child was downright frightening to the old hunter. He stared at the child without moving from the pile of skins that now formed his bed. The odd creature stared back at Quatermain with his gray eyes and hollow cheeks mimicking the old hunter's facial expressions. Its long blonde hair flopped about as the child twisted its head about glaring Quatermain.

"You should eat first," offered Macumazahn.

"I ate my last meal decades ago," answered the child.

"Evidently," responded Quatermain in reference to the sagging skin that hung loosely from the bones of the frail child.

"He-who-see-in-the-dark only looks with his eyes and so my appearance is startling to him. I expected more of a man that has seen so many wondrous things in my country."

Quatermain did not answer but stood to his feet casting off the blanket made from hides and realized that he was naked. "Where are my clothes?"

The child smiled and pointed a single bony digit toward the wall behind Macumazahn. "I need to wake from this dream. I have slumbered way too long."

"It is no dream, Macumazahn. Certainly you have had experiences that were difficult to explain before," argued the wraith like child.

Quatermain chose not to answer him but pulled on a pair of new leather breeches that fit him perfectly. They were golden brown and supple to the touch. On the floor before him were boots, a belt, and a leather shirt all made out of the same golden brown leather as the breeches. His Webley revolver and his knife hung from the belt and the boots fit him as if the finest cobbler in England had handcrafted the shoes just for him.

"Who did this?" asked Quatermain as he turned to face the boy but the child was gone. A large slouch bush hat and a riding cape sat in a neat pile next to the fire. The old hunter would have left the riding cape where it lay had it not been made of the most unusual translucent, white hide with a heavy mane for a collar.

"Sit and eat. You need your strength," spoke Eshu.

"You and the boy are the same person, correct?" asked Quatermain as he sat down in front of the fire.

"Person?"

"You are...the boy and the boy is Eshu?"

"Are you the collector of horns? Are you the watcher-in-the-night? Are you Macumazahn? Or are you Allan Quatermain?"

"I am all of those things or at least I have been called all of those things."

"Then so am I."

Quatermain remembered seeing Umslopogaas lying dead on the floor and he turned quickly to see if his friend was truly dead but there was nothing there where he had laid not even a blood stain. He turned his attention back to the fire and roasted meat that hung from the spit. It didn't appear to be overly charred and the pitcher of milk was in its same place.

"Eat of the flesh of the lion and drink of his milk. You need your strength." Quatermain sat with his back against the wall and carved pieces of meat from the spit with his knife. His hunger was immense as was his thirst. He gobbled down the charred flesh and washed it down with the warm milk. It was unusually refreshing.

"What am I eating?" asked Quatermain.

"You eat the flesh of the lady that was clad in calfskin and encircled in gold. You devourer your lover and drink her blood," called out the child that now sat across from Quatermain by the fire.

Quatermain spit out the piece of meat that was between his teeth and grabbed for the pitcher. The wraith like child laughed uncontrollably as Quatermain looked into the vessel filled and discovered thick, frothy crimson drink. He felt sick to his stomach and would have thrown up his meal had it been possible but it wasn't possible. Whatever was on the spit and in that pitcher was now part of him.

Quatermain turned his head looking once more to where Umslopogaas had been laid before him dead and he saw the woman's beautiful, dead eyes staring back at him. Her dress was removed and she lay there naked with her side torn open. "What did you do to me?" he called out but as he turned the child was gone.

"I haven't done anything to you," whispered the voice of Eshu.

"Where is that demon? That thing that sat here with me? That thing that fed me human flesh disguised as game?"

"No one has done such a thing. Eat, Allan Quatermain. You will need your strength," offered Eshu as his voice resonated within the old hunter's chest.

Quatermain felt himself taken by hunger again and he carved flesh from the spit with his knife as he had done previously. He washed down the bits of meat with milk from the pitcher and was thoroughly refreshed. The hunter leaned his head back against the cavern wall and would have gone to sleep had it not been for the voice of the child disturbing him.

"What have you done this time, Allan Quatermain? You have gnawed on the bones of your friend and have quenched your thirst with his blood."

"I have not," yelled Quatermain at the child. He whipped his head about to where he had seen the body of the woman and to his relief there was nothing there. Quatermain turned to face the child noticing his smirk and that he was staring at his cape. The hunter slowly reached his hands upward and undid the clasp that held the cape in place. He first noticed that the heavy mane collar was missing and then as he whirled it from his shoulders he saw the shriveled head of Umslopogaas dangling from the collar of the cape. He glanced back to the place where the woman had been lying and in her place was Umslopogaas naked and flayed.

Quatermain flew into rage as he leaped to his feet and pulled his revolver from its holster. He squeezed the trigger repeatedly and the hefty rounds sprinted toward the child. "Die! You wicked sot!" yelled the enraged hunter. The bullets crashed into the limestone floor sending sparks and bits of rock into the air but the wraith of a child was gone. Salty tears bathed Quatermain's dirty face as he touched the side of the barrel to his temple and he cradled his head with his other hand. He collapsed to his knees in overwhelming agony of spirit cursing and yelling at the child and at Eshu. Quatermain lifted the revolver again and fired the remaining two bullets into the dark recesses of the cavern. He stood to his feet kicking at the spit and the burning coals only to lose his balance and fall facedown shattering the pitcher of milk. Cut up and bruised, the grieving Quatermain crawled back to the pile of hides and pulled a weighty animal skin over his head. "I need to wake up," groaned Macumazahn.

"If we were smart and cunning men, we would flee like frightened rabbits," sighed Captain John Good.

"I've never been accused of being smart or cunning," laughed Sir Henry Curtis.

"And so we ride into the jaws of hell only to become lodged in its bowels," groaned Good as he watched Bristol load his wagon onto the ferry.

"How many soldiers do you reckon, Curtis?"

"By the number of horses and the innumerable tents, at least 200 soldiers armed with Martinis, maybe more."

"It would appear so," sighed Good.

"You think different?" asked Curtis.

"I know different," laughed Good "there is one large supply tent set up at the center of their camp and only one wagon."

"What does that matter?"

"An expedition of two hundred or more men requires enormous support and substantially more wagons. They have a centrally located tent that serves as their supply tent and command but no auxiliary tents like a mess tent," pointed out Good.

"Get to it man!" exclaimed Curtis.

"This is a cavalry unit of about fifty men. They travel light and strike fast. The extra tents are to intimidate the locals."

"What is a single band of cavalry doing so far south and unsupported?" asked Curtis.

"I don't know but I just imagine that Perkins and Bristol know!" growled Captain John Good.

Curtis drove the team of oxen onto the ferry as the sun slipped just beyond the distant horizon. A single, white cowbird landed on the head of the lead oxen and rested there lazily. The bird crooked its neck and met Sir Henry Curtis' stare. It opened its mouth as if it would say something to Curtis with its yellow beak gaped wide but instead it squawked out its complaint and then shook itself vigorously. Curtis looked up from the bird in time to see Bristol enter the command tent accompanied by Perkins and two men that were part of the cavalry unit.

Sir Henry Curtis landed face down in the stagnant backwater from the flood plain of the Zambezi River that filled the abandoned mine shaft that now served as the brig for Bristol's cavalry unit. Next to him laid Captain John Good who was knocked unconscious in a struggle that ensued after they were escorted out of the Lieutenant's tent and next to him was the emaciated Umslopogaas.

"Incubu, suffers the same indignities as Umslopogaas," whispered the Zulu Chieftain.

Curtis spit and sputtered the rancid water as he struggled to get to his knees. Pungent mud clung to his face and the water dripped from his chin onto his chest. "It is good to see you, friend," gasped Sir Henry Curtis.

"Is it? Is there anything good about this?" asked Umslopogaas.

"We are alive and there is still opportunity to strangle Bristol with his own lying tongue," growled Curtis.

"We aren't alive for long. Tomorrow they begin gladiatorial games and we are to be the contestants," warned Umslopogaas.

"Gladiatorial games?" questioned Curtis as he struggled against his shackles.

"They are to pit us against each other in a fight to the death and that is if we are fortunate," spoke a strange voice from deep within the mineshaft.

Curtis stood to his feet and helped Umslopogaas to stand as a man emerged from the shadows wearing a leather breast plate that was notched and fitted with pieces of bone from just below the neck to his belly button and a leather skirt that resembled a kilt hung from his waist. His feet were bare other than a large gold ring on each toe and several gold ringlets about each ankle. He wore bracers and greaves made of crocodile hide and his long dark hair hung about his face in braids. His name was Chibuike and he was a prince among the Basuto.

"The fortunate?" asked Curtis.

"We are all dead men. If we perish fighting, little else matters," spoke a faint voice from the shadows just inside the entrance of the mine shaft.

"I would rather a swift strike from a warriors' hand than to be gnawed upon by a crocodile or be thrown into a pit of vipers for their amusement," roared Chibuike.

A Maasai warrior stepped from the shadows just far enough that he could be seen by the others. His red tunic clung to his massive shoulders then cascaded loosely about him to the middle of his thigh. It was cinched about his waist with a leather girdle and he was free from all other adornments. "Choice has been removed from our hands," said the Maasai.

Sir Henry Curtis looked down at Captain John Good who lay motionless and bloody on the floor of the mine shaft then he turned and stared at the hollow cheeks and sunken eyes of Umslopogaas in disbelief. They had traversed Africa in search of riches and adventure. They had faced innumerable challenges, biblical plagues, and a host of enemies but had never been so easily disbanded and defeated.

"What is their purpose?" asked Curtis as he knelt down to tend to the injured Good.

"I am Zulu. You are Maasai. You are Basuto. They have captured chieftains and princes for the slaughter," surmised Umslopogaas.

"But to what purpose? Wouldn't these games unite all of Africa against the Royal Army?" asked Curtis.

"Their purpose is of no consequence. The end result will be the same," grumbled Chibuike.

🌻 🌻 🌻

"Allan Quatermain," whispered a soft, gentle voice. "Allan Quatermain, you need to arise from your slumber. Your friends are in need of you." Quatermain awoke with a jolt and sat straight up. Kneeling in front of him was the beautiful, dark skinned woman with long black hair curled in ringlets. Her golden eyes were fixed on his and her full lips were pushed together as she leaned forward and touched them to his forehead. "We all need you, Allan Quatermain," she whispered.

Quatermain started to respond but she touched a single finger to his lips preventing him from speaking then she stood to her feet. Her hands slipped behind her and she undid the clasp that held the calfskin dress in place. Quatermain's eyes widened as he stared at her unveiled, raw beauty. "Who are you?" asked the old hunter.

"I have been called many things and have been many things," she said softly as she knelt once more in front of Macumazahn.

"What do I call you?"

"You have called me many things. You have loved me. You have cursed me. You have sought for me and you have abandoned me. Now you have returned to me," she spoke sternly.

"I've just met you and you say that I have loved you."

"You have loved me and you love me still." She took Quatermain's hands into her own and placed them upon her thighs. "I am Nambi. I am the first woman."

"What is that you want from me?"

"I want what you want."

"I have no idea what I want. I have been here too long. I'm lost."

"You have loved me and you love me still."

"Allan Quatermain," laughed the hideous, frail child "You need to leave this cave."

"Allan Quatermain," roared Eshu "You need to leave this cave."

"I'm losing my mind," shuttered Quatermain.

"They are here to assist you with the task at hand," the voice of the golden eyed woman poured over him like waves crashing upon a shore. Her voice eroded his fears and was like a calming ointment to his wounded spirit.

"What task? What is it that you ask of me?" questioned Macumazahn.

"This land will be torn apart and your friends lost to you forever if you do not act," said Nambi as she placed both hands on his face cradling his cheeks.

"I am wounded and I have been separated from my expedition for many days," mumbled Quatermain.

Nambi pulled the face of Quatermain toward her and laid his cheek against her breast. "You wear the armor of the trickster and I have leant you my strength. Follow the child out of the cave, accept whatever assistance that he may offer, but never return to this place." Allan Quatermain could not resist her command. He stood to his feet and followed the child to the fissure at the mouth of the cave watching his blonde hair sway back and forth across his bony shoulders. Quatermain couldn't help but notice that the child's backbone was evident and that you could count his ribs easily. He wondered what assistance this starved child could provide.

"I'm certain that you will fail and when you fail, I will be there to greet you," proclaimed the wraith like child.

"You find me reprehensible but yet you seek my boon," the child wheezed at Quatermain. "Had it not been for Nambi, I would have never rescued you."

"It was you that saved me from the jaws of the white lion?"

"No. I saved you from yourself," roared the child as he shook himself violently. The child fell to the ground and stretched himself flat against the earth. His body then twisted about writhing in agony as his limbs elongated and his bones broke reforming into something else entirely. Quatermain turned to run hoping to escape back into the cave but the fissure was closed and he stared at the steep mountain face. It was nothing but sheer rock now. He turned to face the child once more only to see horrible fangs and a formidable jaw rip through the abomination's skull as the child's miniscule measure of humanity was swallowed up and a giant beast appeared. Quatermain stared into the face of the White Lion once more.

"How is this possible?" asked Quatermain.

The White Lion shook himself and his translucent mane unfurled like a flag caught up by gale force wind. He roared in defiance of the natural order, in defiance of the heavens, and in defiance of the fates and his pride was gathered to him immediately as if they had been awaiting his call. Quatermain stood on the edge of the crag surrounded by the marauding lions that had nearly ended his life and now they were his allies.

✺ ✺ ✺

Quatermain pressed his back against the cliff wall with his hands spread wide in an attempt to grip its sheer face. He was uncertain of what he had just witnessed and his mind swayed almost to the point of losing consciousness at the thought of the monster's heavy fangs tearing into his flesh once more. He closed his eyes in an effort to steady himself and he was overcome with a longing to see Umslopogaas, to hear the roar of Sir Henry Curtis' laughter, and to watch Captain John Good preen and strut in front of an unencumbered lady. He missed his friends and thought how dreadful it would be to die on this crag alone.

"You must leave this place with haste or everything will be lost." It was the voice of Nambi, the first woman, swirling about him carried by the warm south wind and it soothed his fears.

"How am I to leave this place?"

The abominable beast lunged forward and struck Allan Quatermain with his snout in the stomach. His fear of the beast was quelled by the words of Nambi resounding in his mind. "Accept whatever assistance that he may offer," he mumbled to himself. It showed its yellow, stained teeth in what can only be described as an awful grin and nudged Quatermain a second time lifting him from the ground with his snout. Macumazahn clutched at his mane with both hands in an attempt not to lose his balance. His legs sprawled about wildly as the lion lifted him up toward the sky when it occurred to him that the lion was trying to lift him onto his back. Quatermain swung his leg over the animal and gripped the beard of the lion with both hands.

"Bloody hell," yelled Macumazahn as the white lion dove over the precipice of the crag and plummeted toward the floor of the gorge. The beast landed on all fours with an earth-rending crash that created tremors and cascading waves of dirt and rock in every direction. It then bellowed in an otherworldly voice calling all nearby lions to his side.

"Stop those men that would rape this land and destroy its people," whispered Nambi to him in an echo from the distant crag.

"Get me to Bristol," whispered Macumazahn to the abomination and the beast sprinted forward bounding over the ridge heading north toward the Zambezi River.

✻ ✻ ✻

"Sir Henry Curtis, our country will mourn your loss but to die in service to Queen and country is the greatest of honors," shouted Bristol to the crowd. "Your sacrifice will not soon be forgotten."

"This is the first battle in a series of contests to determine who the true prince of South Africa is and who has the rightful claim to the famed axe, Inkosi-kass," roared Bristol. He nodded to the guards that held Curtis and they shoved him from the platform into the pit below.

"How am I supposed to fight with my hands bound?" roared Curtis.

"You aren't supposed to fight. You are supposed to die," remarked Perkins from a high back chair that was positioned at the edge of the fighting pit. He sat under a canopy that was intended to protect his blanched skin from the scalding African sun and beside him stood a porter that was armed with a broad headed spear. Perkins nibbled at a black plum but did not find it to his liking and spat most of it on the ground. "Get on with it, now!" Perkins shouted.

The mob of tribesman began to cry out and beat their chest in excitement as a large cage was rolled to the edge of the pit by several porters. Curtis shielded his eyes from the sun with his bound hands in an effort to see what was in the cage but all that he could ascertain was that it wasn't human. A latch was released and the gate to the cage swung open facing the fighting pit. All at once the porters lifted the cage and spilled a spotted beast into the pit. It screamed out in anger with a harrowing cry and then it caught the scent of Curtis. His scrapes and cuts filled the leopard's nostrils with the scent of fresh blood and the big cat crouched low baring its fangs.

"I'm going to beat you to death with my bare hands when I get out of here," cursed Curtis.

"You aren't getting out of that pit alive," laughed Perkins. "But please don't die too quickly, we do want everyone to be entertained."

Curtis circled the edge of the pit as the leopard slinked forward still crouched low to the ground and ready to pounce. All of the tribesmen began to chant and stomp their feet in rhythm in an indiscernible tongue.

"They are worshiping the leopard, Mr. Curtis. The beast is sacred to them. So consider yourself an offering to appease the gods and the natives," laughed Perkins.

"I'm going to hate to disappoint them," chided Curtis.

Then suddenly the leopard leaped forward with its claws outstretched aiming for Sir Henry Curtis' throat. Curtis lifted his bound hands and caught the beast just below the neck but the force of the animal's assault drove him to the ground. Man and beast were entangled in a violent struggle as the leopard's claws tore at Curtis' shoulders and its jaws snapped shut just inches from his face. Curtis pulled his knee underneath the belly of the beast and angled his shin against the animal separating himself from death by a hair for a breath. It was the moment that Curtis needed to employ his remarkable strength to flip the beast off him and into the wall of the pit directly behind him. The leopard crashed into the hewn rock wall with a thud and slowly staggered to its feet disoriented and wondering how its quarry had escaped.

Curtis was up on his feet instantly and steadied himself for the animal's next attack when Perkins called out to Bristol, "Shoot him. Shoot him." Bristol pulled his revolver from its holster and squeezed the trigger. The leopard crumpled to the ground without even a twitch. It was a clean kill.

"What did you do?" called out Perkins in an outrage.

"You said shoot him…so I shot him," responded Bristol. "Certainly, you wouldn't have meant to kill Sir Henry Curtis in such a cowardly manner."

"Letting that man live is mistake," Perkins sniveled.

"He's wounded. If the wounds don't fester and kill him, I'm sure you'll discover another way for the man to meet his end," waned Bristol as he stared at Curtis. The injured Incubu nodded at Bristol as merely an acknowledgement that he chose to disobey Perkins and not shoot him. It wasn't a "thank you" or a gesture of goodwill because Curtis had every intention of killing Bristol when he had opportunity. It was merely a nod.

Curtis reached down and picked up the carcass of the leopard throwing it over his shoulder easily and climbed out of the pit. He was led back to the flooded mine and forced inside.

Macumazahn gripped the mane of the white lion and squeezed tightly around its torso with his legs as the enormous beast hurtled across the South African plains. He listened intently for the voice of Nambi or for that of Eshu but all he could hear was the bellowing of the white lion and the other beasts responding to his call. The number of lions had doubled since the beast had sprinted across the ridge where they had initially set up their encampment. It was a spectacle that is difficult to describe and much harder to comprehend. Quatermain thought to himself that a more deadly army could not have been assembled without raising the dead or conjuring all of hell. Then he had a disturbing thought, he wondered what would be the cost of having received help from Nambi, Eshu, and the little boy, who he was certain was death, Himself.

"You keep my friends alive and I will gladly pay the price for your assistance," yelled the old hunter at the beast that he rode. The white lion did not respond but lowered his head and sprinted forward at even a greater pace than before.

"Umslopogaas, the usurper, the thief, the bastard son of the Zulu people is here to defend his claim to Inkosi-kass," barked Bristol. "He is to face a true son of the Zulu nation. A man who deserves to hold Inkosi-kass. He is to do battle with Nomzamo."

Bristol motioned with his head for the contestants to enter the fighting pit and without hesitation Nomzamo leaped from the platform into the hewn pit. Umslopogaas struggled against the soldiers that led him to the platform for no other reason that he resented a man putting his hand on him. They had restrained the Zulu chieftain's hands by binding his wrist together but they should have considered binding his feet as well.

"Throw him in the pit, now!" yelled Perkins impatiently.

As they neared the edge, Umslopogaas kicked the feet out from under the guard that held onto his right arm and the soldier landed soundly on his back. The Zulu chieftain shoved the second soldier violently knocking him to the ground just as the first guard made it to his feet.

"I am Umslopogaas. I am the slaughterer. I am the mighty Woodpecker. Never lay your hand on me again," he screamed as he kicked the guard. Perkins cursed and ordered men to seize Umslopogaas, but his voice could not be heard because of the shouts of the spectators. Umslopogaas, who was believed to be attempting to escape, instead leaped into the pit after the guard and landed with both feet on the soldier's neck. The soldier gasped for a brief moment clawing at the ground as he suffered a crushed windpipe but Umslopogaas brought a swift end to his life by crushing his skull with his foot.

Nomzamo gazed at Umslopogaas pensively and then spoke to him in the Zulu tongue. He then bowed his head to Umslopogaas but the Zulu chieftain did not return the gesture. Nomzamo turned toward the platform behind him and one of the soldiers tossed a broad headed spear down to him. Umslopogaas turned to face the crowd of spectators behind but no one offered him a weapon and his hands were still bound.

"Nomzamo, your prince, versus Umslopogaas, the traitor of your people. Let the battle begin," yelled Bristol over the clamors of the crowd.

Nomzamo held his spear up with one hand and walked toward Umslopogaas slowly. The Zulu chieftain understood the gesture and held his hands out. Nomzamo cut loose the bindings from Umslopogaas' wrist and then backed away slowly never taking his eyes off of his opponent. Those surrounding the pit yelled out in anger while others commended the young prince.

"A man of honor," Umslopogaas said as he motioned toward Nomzamo. "These men are serpents and they would have us kill one another for their own purposes." Umslopogaas pointed at Perkins and said, "You that are gathered here should throw him into the pit." The crowd clamored in support of Umslopogaas' argument but no one moved toward Perkins.

"You are the one that brought the Englishmen to their land. You have always aided the white man and abandoned your own people. That is why no one comes to your aid or listens to your commands. The mighty Umslopogaas," snarled Perkins.

"Fight," yelled Bristol.

Umslopogaas turned to face Nomzamo with his knees bent and his arms forming a semi-circle in almost a wrestler's stance. Nomzamo raised the spear overhead shouting to the spectators in his native tongue and then he brought the spear down violently across his knee breaking it half. Nomzamo picked up both pieces holding them overhead and howled at the crowd as he waved his hands above his head. The spectators became frantic calling out their approval for the young prince in one fashion or another.

"Fight cannot be fair," said Nomzamo.

"It never is," called back Umslopogaas.

"You will have a weapon though," answered Nomzamo as tossed part of the broken haft at Umslopogaas' feet.

Umslopogaas picked up the haft and pointed out that his end was without a spearhead and Nomzamo and Umslopogaas laughed together. "The fight cannot be fair," roared Nomzamo.

"It never is," laughed Umslopogaas.

The two men circled each other in the large, hewn out cistern where their kinsmen had gathered to watch them slay one another. Nomzamo lunged forward first in haste and Umslopogaas took advantage of his youth and inexperience. The Zulu chieftain deflected Nomzamo's attack by striking the prince's wrist pushing the blade wide and nearly knocking it loose from Nomzamo's grip. Umslopogaas struck the prince hard in the side with the haft crushing Nomzamo's ribs as the prince stumbled past him trying to regain his balance from his poorly executed attack.

"You should have given me the spearhead," grunted Umslopogaas as he tossed the haft back and forth between his hands.

"I should have placed it to my own throat as well, I'm guessing," responded Nomzamo as he wheezed trying to catch his breath.

"It would have made for less suffering," smirked Umslopogaas.

Nomzamo sprang forward with unexpected prowess swinging the blade first left then right in sweeping across-the-body motions that caused the Zulu chieftain to retreat backwards in an effort to escape the sharp edge. Umslopogaas backpedaled until he reached the stone wall and then he dove forward in a roll and struck Nomzamo violently in the lower leg with the haft as he went past. The prince fell to the ground in agony with a bone protruding out of his shin. "The fight cannot be fair," pontificated Umslopogaas.

"It never is," grunted Nomzamo.

The Zulu prince struggled to his feet and peered over his shoulder at his kinsmen. He didn't say anything but there was an evident sadness in his countenance. Nomzamo let his gaze linger but just a moment and then straightened himself to meet Umslopogaas once more. He reversed his grip on his blade and held it pointing outward with his palm facing down. His only hope was for Umslopogaas to make an unwise charge impaling himself upon the spear.

"This is what trusting men like Perkins brings to our people," yelled out Umslopogaas. "He murders your prince. He brings war to this land."

Umslopogaas dove into a forward shoulder roll and struck Nomzamo with a violent blow to the opposite shin and it sent the Zulu prince shrieking to the ground. The Zulu chieftain then walked behind Nomzamo as he wallowed on the clay floor in agony and dropped his knee into the middle of the prince's back. He slipped the haft under the chin of Nomzamo and yanked backwards with a primal yell breaking Nomzamo's neck and the prince fell to the ground dead.

"This is what these men have brought," called out Umslopogaas.

"Nomzamo fought bravely as a noble prince but it was this beast that took his life," offered Perkins. "Kill Umslopogaas," ordered Perkins and Bristol pulled his revolver from its holster and aimed it at the chest of the Zulu chieftain.

"Ready your weapons," ordered Bristol and all of his cavalry unit pulled their revolvers from their holsters and aimed them at Umslopogaas. "Fire," yelled Bristol. Flame belched out of their barrels in a raucous roar as Bristol's men squeezed the trigger on their weapons but at the last moment they had aimed their revolvers into the crowd instead of at Umslopogaas and killed hundreds of the natives that had gathered to watch the spectacle.

"No," yelled Perkins as he leaped to his feet in protest of the massacre.

Bristol calmly turned to face Perkins as the next wave of gunfire ripped through the crowd and pointed his revolver at the chubby, pink, freckled politician. He pulled the trigger and the weighty round tore through Perkins chest. "You were never giving the orders here," muttered Bristol. "These are my men. These will always be my men," Bristol continued as Perkins slumped into back into his chair. Another round of gunfire exploded and more men died as Bristol pulled the trigger back once more shooting Perkins in the head. "This was always my plan," lauded Bristol.

Frantic, horrible cries echoed to the heavens as gallons of blood seeped into the ground. The White Lion had reached the bank of the Zambezi River just as Perkins slumped into his chair. Forced by dark, obscure magic the lions leaped into the river and swam across without hesitation as Macumazahn rode across safely on the back of the enormous, pale beast. He pulled his Winchester repeater from his back and leaped down from his mount firing at Bristol's soldiers as they came into view. The white lion disappeared into the smoke and confusion seeking out the vicious, unstable men that thought to tear his land apart.

Quatermain eased his way into the maze of tents sending forth a gale of bullets each one finding their target as the lions tore both animal and soldier into shreds. Bristol and his men mounted little resistance to the sudden and unexpected attack. They died, all of them. All of them except Bristol, who the white lion had sought out and pinned down for Allan Quatermain.

"Quatermain, I thought you were dead," offered Bristol in utter terror.

"Thank God that you are alive. The savages went insane and attacked our soldiers. They killed Perkins and most likely your men."

"Savages?" asked Quatermain as slung his rifle over his shoulder and picked up a revolver from one of the fallen cavalry.

"Yes, the savages. They murdered everyone," Bristol repeated. "Help me, kill this beast. The natives must be controlling these lions with some sort of voodoo."

"Voodoo?" asked Quatermain.

"Help me man. Please," begged Bristol.

Umslopogaas emerged from the chaos with Curtis at his side carrying a wounded but alive Captain John Good. Their faces spread into smile when they saw the old hunter standing over Bristol with his revolver in his hand.

"I told you, Curtis, Macumazahn is not so easily killed," grunted Umslopogaas.

"Save me. Save me from the lion," cried out Bristol.

"What lion?" asked Curtis.

"He's gone mad. He thinks that the white lion has a hold of him," laughed Quatermain.

"The lions. The lions killed my men. They attacked our horses. This thing is going to kill me," screamed Bristol.

"Your men turned on one another killing each other and some of the tribesman. They are all dead," responded Quatermain matter-of-factly. "Place him in shackles," ordered Macumazahn. A large porter that had stood beside Perkins chair stepped forward and secured Bristol. He smiled a wide grin at Quatermain and he seemed vaguely familiar to the old hunter.

"We are taking you back to England to stand trial for treason," stated Quatermain.

❋ ❋ ❋

Sir Henry Curtis had worked diligently for two weeks with the assistance Umslopogaas in assembling an expedition to travel along the Zambezi River to where Dr. Livingston had been laid to rest deep within the interior of Africa. Captain John Good had returned to the coast with Lieutenant Bristol as his prisoner in hopes of securing passage back to England. Good wasn't healed completely but he felt it was his responsibility to carry Bristol to justice. Allan Quatermain departed from the encampment at the

Zambezi River shortly after Good had left for England. Sir Henry Curtis had tried to convince Macumazahn to travel with them on up river but the old hunter insisted that he had pressing unfinished business. It wasn't until Curtis and Umslopogaas had traveled for many days that Curtis inquired of Umslopogaas what Quatermain's unfinished business might be. Umslopogaas shrugged and answered, "Africa. He searches for her."

THE END

RESEARCH & WRITING

The character of Allan Quatermain appealed to me for one very base reason and that was simply that Quatermain smacks everything that is deemed unacceptable by today's politically correct generation. Greenpeace, vegans, and the sorted lot of political activists would have had a field day with our Victorian Era adventurer. So that made this piece a great deal of fun to write.

I absolutely fell in love with Umslopogaas, the Zulu Chieftain, which has accompanied Quatermain on other adventures. He's intelligent, witty, and can be downright vicious in battle. I would have liked to explore the idea further of Umslopogaas being trapped in England at the bequest of Quatermain while struggling to fit into the mold of a strange society with odd customs. I particularly enjoyed him stepping into the study wearing a coat, tie, and his Zulu leather skirt.

Since this particular story took place in Africa during the 19th century, it required a great deal of research especially for its word count. Maps, weapon diagrams, and the various tribes of South Africa were just a few of the things I spent time delving into. I really hope you have enjoyed reading this tale as much as I enjoyed bringing it together.

DEWAYNE DOWERS - lives on a small farm nestled in the midst of the Ouachita Mountains with his wife, Ann Marie, of 23 years and two beautiful children. He graduated from the University of Arkansas with a degree in Psychology before there were laptops, cell phones, or the internet. DeWayne proudly served his country during Desert Storm. He enjoys authentic Louisiana cuisine, Brazilian Jiu-jitsu, and playing with his wolf-dog Leah. It is rumored that he maintains a secret identity as a project manager for an industrial maintenance group. Follow DeWayne Dowers on Instagram @thedecided

THE UNHOLY ALLIANCE

BY
WAYNE CAREY

I Allan Quatermain, had been a hunter and trader for most of my life, until circumstances changed and Providence brought Sir Henry Curtis and Captain John Good into my life, but that is another story. The one I am about to relate happened many years before, when my dear friend and servant since my youth, Hans the Hottentot, and I ventured too far to the north east in search of ivory. At that time, ivory was a precious commodity greatly desired by the rest of the world. I happened to be good at my job of tracking and shooting the poor beasts whose misfortune it was to bear the magnificent tusks that were in such high demand. Trading in furs and other merchandise among the kraals of Natal, Zululand, and the Transvaal could provide for a meager living, but the occasional cache of ivory kept food on the table. But this particular hunt led to devastating results.

In Pretoria, we outfitted two oxen-drawn wagons and hired our ten men to accompany us, then headed eastward. A drought had scourged the land, chasing away all sorts of game, making it difficult even to keep our party fed. After days of not sighting any elephant spore, I decided on a whim to detour south into Swaziland and pay a visit to the Black Kloof, much to Hans' dissatisfaction.

"Oh, Baas," he would argue every so often after my intentions were realized, "why would you seek out that old wizard. He has brought us nothing but pain. He plays us as one does a puppet on strings."

I could not answer him, so I would only tell him to shut up once his protestations got on my nerves. In truth, I did not know why I wanted to seek out Zikali. I had known him since my youth, and despite his manipulation of people and events toward his own agenda, I found myself looking fondly upon the old, ugly dwarf. He claimed to talk with spirits, to do magic, and to see future events. I believed none of it. What I did believe was that he had an elaborate network of spies who fed him information. The knowledge he gained from anonymous sources had proved useful in the past, and I was willing to risk asking a favor of him with the understanding that I may have to repay it in kind at some future date. But I was already near the bottom of my savings and there seemed to be no respite in sight. I was desperate and willing to withstand Zikali's ridicule and manipulation if he could help in this moment of need.

The Black Kloof, where Zikali lived, was a dreadful, inhospitable place that fostered nightmares. I left the wagons in the care of Hans, who refused to approach the kloof, and went alone, carrying a wooden crate that had been given to me by a customer in Maritzburg instead of payment. I had taken the china tea set to Pretoria in an attempt to sell it, had not found a buyer, so it remained in my wagon. I did not think Zikali would appreciate such frivolity, but I had the urge to take it as a gift rather than a knife or something more practical. Entering the old wizard's kraal, I regretted my decision and felt rather silly carrying the offering.

Without a word, his two enormous servants escorted me to a small fire in front of his hut. It was the middle of the day, not a cloud in the sky, yet the high cliff cast deep shadows that made it seem like a chilly overcast evening. The setting was one that inspired supernatural images in the minds of visitors, nursed by the old dwarf himself, and I was not immune to the effect.

One of the servants held out his hands, nodding toward the crate I held. I passed it over to him and started to say something about it being a gift, but he turned away and walked toward the hut. For some time I stood in front of that fire. It was a hot day, and I had just walked a quarter of a mile, which drenched my shirt and jacket with sweat, but I felt a chill the fire could not chase away.

Presently, the servant crawled out of the hut and motioned me to enter.

In the center of the hut, in front of a circle of embers, Zikali sat on a carved wooden stool, an ancient dwarf with a huge head covered his long, white braids. His eyes glowed red from the coals. A smile twisted his lips. In his hands he held the saucer and cup of fine china. On a stand next to him sat the steaming tea pot and another cup.

"Ah, Macumazahn, welcome," he said in his booming voice. "Come, join me in a cup of tea. Darjeeling. An Englishman who had paid me a visit a year ago had given it to me. Thank you, Macumazahn, for your thoughtful gift. Now I can properly enjoy the tea. Come, sit with me and have some."

I took the stool across from him and accepted the cup his servant passed to me. He poured from the pot, gently set it down, and departed from the hut.

I took a sip, wondering how I should broach the subject I came to discuss.

"So, Macumazahn," he said after sipping from his cup, "you travel so far out of your way to visit this old cheat to ask a favor. Ho, am I some village witch to be bribed with pretty gifts to reveal secrets of the spirit world? No, you do not believe in those spirits, yet you come seeking my advice. You would seek my wisdom, yet deny where that wisdom comes from."

"I know you have many people who pass along information," I said.

"My spies," he said, nodding. "But you think they are all flesh and blood. Does not your own Christian belief tell you of the spirits, both good and bad? There is much in this world that cannot be seen. I have been cursed to see this spiritual realm, to travel it. I am the Opener of Roads. Did you think those were roads of dirt? Hah! But you did not come for a spiritual discussion. You are in need, Macumazahn. You look for a fortune, perhaps? Oh, that will come to you some day, but many years and many heartaches from now. You seek knowledge for the hunt, so that you will not starve in the coming winter. Very well, I will help you as you have helped me, and will help me again later."

I frowned behind my upraised tea cup, knowing that this was his way of saying that I must reciprocate this favor at some later date. I was in his debt, and I almost stopped him so that I would have no need to pay him back, but I was desperate.

"I'm trying to find an elephant herd," I said, lowering my cup to the saucer in my left hand. "This drought hasn't helped. We haven't found any spoor, and I thought some of your contacts might have knowledge of a herd not too far away."

"My spies," he said. "Do you think my spies have nothing better to do than follow elephant herds across the veldt? No, no. The rise of Cetawayo and the decline of Mpande, or the expansion of your colonies and conflicts with the Boers, these are of no interest to them. They would rather follow wildebeest and antelope."

"That's not what I meant," I said, my ire rising.

He laughed heartily. "Macumazahn, do not feel slighted. My spies, as you call them, see all things. Your governor, the great king Cetawayo, even your humble labors, for they know I am fond of you, my friend. I know your troubles, and a nice collection of ivory would keep your belly full for a time. I will tell you how to find a good size herd, but I must warn you also. If you follow this herd, you will find great treasure in ivory, but you will also come to great heartache. You will be faced with a choice. But I know your heart, my friend. The choice would not be difficult for you. So let me tell you first, before I tell you where to find this magnificent herd, that there is an old saying among the Zulu. Do not put all your eggs in one basket."

He tilted his head back and laughed.

I tired of his cryptic talk and regretted my coming here for his advice, but he gave me a location where I might find a herd, and then bent his head and seemed to go to sleep. His servant came and loomed over me, so I got to my feet and left.

I give no stock to Zikali's supernatural claims, but he had a way of being right all of the time. I followed his directions eastward, through the mountains, and when I came upon the herd of over a hundred elephants, I felt a sense of disappointment. It would have been satisfying to go back to the Black Kloof and complain that he had been wrong. Although, knowing Zikali, he would have turned it around and blamed it on my inability to follow simple directions. However, there they were, splendid specimens, peacefully flowing over the grassy hills, pushing down ever tree they came across and defoliating every branch. They devastated the mealie fields surrounding a nearby kraal, consuming what had survived the miserable lack of rain, and the natives made feeble attempts at fending them off. Already in a chaotic struggle with the herd, they were fearful of our approach. Sending one of my men ahead, I made our intentions known, and they were pleased for our help to rid them of the nuisance.

After a few days, more than a dozen were killed and butchered. The tusks were loaded into our wagons and everything else was taken by the locals.

The attack came when we were winding our way through a mountain pass, heading back toward distant Natal.

It was near evening, the sun having slipped behind the mountains and leaving us in gloomy twilight. The first gun shots struck my lead ox but did not kill it. Frightened, the wounded animal bolted, taking the rest of the team along. They ran up the slope, among the rocks, stumbling. The wagon bounced, tilted, and smashed one front wheel. It tipped, the team wrenching free, and overturned. When the reins were pulled from my hands, I fell backward off the box. The wagon rolled around me, crashing and splintering, burying me under a pile of shattered wood, supply crates, and ivory tusks. From underneath the wreckage, I could see the stumbling oxen. The leader dropped over, dead or dying. Gunshots tore into the others, stopping their struggles.

My head ached. Pain surged through me, blurring my vision. I feared many bones had been broken. I could not move to retrieve one of my rifles to fend off the attack. I could not even reach the revolver at my side. I was pinned under the broken wagon and all the supplies and half the ivory cargo, helpless as I listened to the sounds of a battle raging around me. It would have been one-sided, since my men were unarmed. Even Hans did not carry a weapon other than a knife. The rifles were stored in the wagons and I doubted any of them had enough time to reach them.

"*Não os mate!*" someone kept shouting.

My muddled brain tried to make sense of the words. It sounded like so much gibberish. Not English and not Zulu, and I ran through the other languages I have known or have heard over the years as I struggled to remain conscious. The world around me kept fading, but I refused to die without so much as a fight, meager though it might be. I pushed and pulled to free myself, my head swimming with every movement, blood from some cut on my scalp blinding me.

The shouting came again. Not French or Dutch, but I had heard its like before.

Portuguese!

But by then the sounds echoed hollowly around me. I spun wildly into darkness.

I did not die then, obviously, as I thought I would. When the morning came, it brought my senses and a great deal of pain. I took stock of my situation. By flexing fingers and toes, I determined that nothing appeared to be broken, as I had feared, but I was severely bruised. The cut on my head had stopped bleeding and was throbbing. I was still pinned beneath the remains of my wagon, but I was alive.

I began to push some of the debris from me, little by little. It felt as though I were moving an ocean, one drop of water at a time.

Presently, a shadow cast away the sunlight streaming though the opening in the wreckage. Then a face appeared.

"Macumazahn?"

"Here!" I said, my voice croaking.

"It is I, Uuka. I will get you out."

The task might be too much for one person, though Uuka was a big man. "Where are the others?" I asked.

"Gone," he said, his voice lower that I barely heard it. "All gone."

I did not know what he meant by this remark and I was afraid to ask him for clarity.

An hour he worked, moving bits of the broken wagon off of me until he could use one long plank as a lever to lift the bulk of it so that I could wiggle out. Uuka cleaned the wound on my head and applied some medicine from our supplies. It was not a deep cut and my hat covered it and kept a small bandage in place. Sitting beside the ruined wagon, with the oxen all laying dead not far away, I drank some water, ate some biltong, and gathered my strength and my wits.

"Now, Uuka, tell me what happened."

He squatted beside me, looking at the ground. "Many men, with rifles. They charged down at us. They shot your oxen, causing your wagon to overturn. They shot at the other one that Hans drove. All the men ran in every direction."

"Hans?" I asked, fearing his answer.

"He was not shot. He jumped into the back of the wagon and got a rifle that was behind the box. He started shooting, but they swarmed over the wagon and beat him. They chased some men down. I ran too, Macumazahn. I am sorry. We are not warriors, like the Zulu. We are only laborers. I ran to the top of that hill and hid. I watched them take Hans and tie him up and throw him into the back of the wagon. Then they turned the oxen around and went back through the pass. After they were gone, I came down and found you still alive."

"Then Hans was alive," I said.

"Yes, Macumazahn."

I pushed myself up, my legs still aching. "Then we must go after him."

"No, Macumazahn. There are too many of them. Fifteen or twenty, I could not count them. All with guns."

"White men?" I asked.

"Only half were white. They kept yelling in a strange language. They were all mean men."

"I thought I heard Portuguese."

Uuka only shrugged.

"Did they capture anyone else?" I asked.

"Three of our men. Tied their hands and then put nooses around their necks and tied them to the back of the wagon. They did not hunt the rest of us down. They were happy with the wagon."

"And the ivory," I said. "But why didn't they loot this wagon? Half the ivory is in it."

"They seemed to be in a hurry. That is why they did not hunt the rest of us. Some of the white men called them all back. It all took very little time."

I took stock of the destroyed wagon and started picking through the crates of supplies.

"We'll take two rifles each, and plenty of ammunition, and as much supplies as we can carry. No telling how long it will take to follow them."

"Follow them!" Uuka's voice squeaked. His eyes bulged in shock. "We cannot follow them. They are slavers. They will kill you because you are white and not worth anything, and they will tie me up and sell me."

"Exactly why we need to find them and rescue Hans and the others."

"But there are thirty of them," he insisted.

I pulled out one of my express rifles, but the barrel had been bent from the crash. Tossing it aside, I was able to find a new Martini Henry undamaged. I handed it to Uuka and found a second.

"A moment ago," I said, "there were only fifteen or twenty. Now there's thirty of them?"

He shrugged. "Who can count heads when they are shooting at you? There are more than two. We are outnumbered no matter what."

I pulled free a box of ammunition, stood, and glared at Uuka. "I will not leave Hans to that fate. I have known him since I was a boy. He would not desert me, I will not desert him. You do not need to come with me, Uuka. I was paying you only to hunt elephants. I will give you what I owe you, so you may go if you want."

Uuka frowned and stared at his worn sandals and dirty feet. Presently he bit his lip and shook his head. "I will go with you, Macumazahn. You may pay me … if we live."

I returned to the wagon and tugged one of the tusks out of the way.

"What about the ivory?" he asked, reaching in and pulling on another tusk.

"What about it?" I asked. It seemed a silly question. With just two of us, we certainly couldn't carry even one each, let alone the whole cache.

"You do not want it left here, so that anyone might stumble upon it."

"Well, we can't take any of it with us," I said.

He pointed down the way we had come, the direction in which the Portuguese had taken Hans and the others. "We passed a cave. We can hide them there, then cover the opening."

"I don't want to waste any time," I said. "Hang the ivory."

"I will move the ivory while you gather the supplies," he said. "You know what we can take and what will be necessary, I do not. Let me hide the tusks."

I acquiesced.

As he began to drag the first of the tusks, a thought came to me. I found a shovel and tossed it toward him. "Put all but two tusks in the cave. Keep the best two out and bury them nearby. It won't do to put all our eggs in one basket."

He gave me a puzzled look, but nodded.

It frustrated me as to how long it took to gather our supplies and to make ready our hunt. I loaded packs with ammunition for two Martini Henrys and my revolver as well as a good supply of biltong, dried game meat that we had stored in the wagon. There were also some skins filled with water. No tents, but a bedroll for each of us. I did not care for Uuka to waste his time dragging the tusks into hiding. They meant nothing to me if I could not find Hans and the others. I left him to it, knowing that each moment we delayed, the Portuguese traders were slipping further away, and on one of *my* wagons. If they had just taken the wagon and the cargo of ivory it carried, I would not have bothered. But Hans was a member of my family. Annoying, at times a drunkard, but always loyal. He had saved my life many times. The other men I did not know at all, except for this trip, but they were in my charge and under my protection. They were my responsibility.

Uuka returned, wiping dust from his hands, his threadbare shirt plastered to his broad back and chest with sweat.

I handed him a pack and one of the rifles, and we started our journey.

We came out of the pass and followed the tracks of my stolen wagon over the grassy hills. So intent on the trail was I that I did not see a party coming from the north until they were within a quarter of a mile. At first I thought they were the Portuguese, circling back, but I saw no wagon, only a single horse and rider and several dozen men on foot. A spyglass would have been helpful to learn their identity, but I had discarded mine because of broken lenses and bent casing. The fact that there was one man on horseback suggested a European, perhaps a Boer, but it could also be another Portuguese. Despite seeing the rider, I had a terrible foreboding.

"*Inkosi*," Uuka said, "we should run."

"Where?" I demanded.

There was nowhere to hide and though we had enough ammunition to take on this group, we would be overrun before we could shoot and reload less than three or four times. We stood our ground as the horseman broke off from the rest of his party and galloped toward us.

Robes flowed behind him as he rode. So he was Arab. As he drew closer, I noticed his thick curly beard and dark complexion. His robes and head wrap were of bright cloth and rich fabric. He was not an ordinary Arab trader, but one of apparent wealth, although his dark skin suggested that he was of mixed heritage.

He reined his horse in front of us, grinning down at me, unconcerned that we carried weapons. I could have easily drawn my revolver and killed him, but he had from thirty to fifty men at his back. He seemed to know that this was enough threat to ensure his safety. Either that or he was a very arrogant man.

"Englishman," he said in a thick accent. "You are far from home. Are you the hunter I heard of who has come to this land?"

"I am Allan Quatermain," I said.

He pursed his bearded lips and nodded. "I have heard of you, Hunter Quatermain. And I am Prince Abdullah bin Majid, son of the late Sultan of Zanzibar, nephew to the present Sultan. Tell me, Hunter Quatermain, how is it that you are here with but a single servant and look to be the worst for wear? You have been in a recent struggle, I am guessing."

"Yes, Prince Abdullah," I said, bowing my head in a show of courtesy. Although I suspected that he was a prince only through one of the late sultan's concubines, it would not do to anger him. A demonstration of respect would go a long way. "Our party was raided by Portuguese traders."

His face turned to disgust and he spat upon the ground. "Portuguese!" He then spoke in his native tongue words that I was vaguely familiar with and were not used in proper company.

Then he beamed at me again. "Come, join us. You are my guest. We shall camp near the stream that is just over that rise. We shall feast on fresh meat and you shall tell me of your woes."

"With all due respect, Prince Abdullah," I said, "I would like to continue after these raiders. I have already lost time in pursuing them."

"Nonsense. I see that you follow the trail of a wagon. Yours? Stolen by these thieves? The trail will still be there in the morning. Night is falling and you must rest. You, my friend, look as though you can barely stand. You will rest in your own tent tonight, upon soft furs, with a full belly, as my guest. I will take no argument, Hunter Quatermain. It is decided."

He pulled the reins, turned his horse around and kicked its ribs to spur it into a gallop back to his long line of men.

"We should not stay, Macumazahn," Uuka said. "I do not like this one. He smiles too much."

"I don't think it would be a good idea to spurn his offer of hospitality," I said. "He is not someone we should anger. I don't want to delay our pursuit of those who took Hans, but I can't see that we have any choice."

By the time the sun was setting, Abdullah's people had erected two tents on the top of a hill overlooking the stream. Fires were burning and an antelope that had been killed only hours before was roasting. One tent was huge, larger than my humble house in Durban, with many partitions,

"Come, join us. You are my guest."

and I wondered how all the rugs and cloths and poles were carried by men alone. The smaller tent was provided for me, where I was presented with bowls of water from the stream with which to bathe. My torn and soiled clothes were taken to be washed, and fortunately I had a second pair of trousers and a spare shirt rolled up in my pack. Wrinkled as they were, they were at least clean. With the use of some scented oils the prince provided, I was presentable for his feast.

Uuka haunted my every move, his eyes fearful. He had tried to enter into conversation with some of the prince's servants who provided me with cleaning supplies and water, but each remained silent, with downcast eyes.

Two armed Arabs came to escort me to Abdullah's tent. Uuka made to follow, but they insisted he remain behind. One spoke vehemently in Arabic and made his wishes known through gestures, going so far as to draw a curved dagger and wave it in Uuka's face. Uuka backed into my tent and sat down on the rugs to glumly await my return.

The sun had dropped, plunging the hills into night, the darkness alleviated by torches and small fires. One Arab parted the tent flap and the second ushered me inside. The rich rugs were laden with cushions and furs surrounding silver plates and bowls filled with a variety of foods. The roasted antelope filled the tent with an aroma that made my poor empty belly grumble with anticipation. There were fresh fruits, dried fruits, nuts.

My escort motioned to a particular pile of pillows, and I dropped my aching body among them.

Abdullah swaggered in from another part of the tent, tossing back a curtain and slapping his hands together.

I struggled to rise, knowing that some people who pretend royalty are very particular as to protocol and the demonstration of respect. Abdullah, however, waved me back.

"Relax, my friend. We do not stand upon ceremonies here. You and I, we are equals out here. We are both traders and hunters, although you have a greater reputation in the former than I could ever hope for."

"And I can imagine by your grand appearance, Prince Abdullah, that you are a much better trader than I can ever hope to be," I said.

He laughed as he squatted down among the cushions.

Two servants, black men in white robes, brought in bowls of fragrant water and towels, tending to each of us as we washed. Then Abdullah took a large piece of roasted meat from a plate and tore into it, saying around his full mouth, "Come, eat. Do not let this marvelous beast go to waste."

Another servant brought in two silver goblets and a goatskin filled with wine. He bowed, offering one cup to the prince, uncorked the skin, and filled the cup. Then he passed the second to me and filled it. He never looked at me, his eyes ever downcast.

"Thank you," I said.

I saw him hesitate before he withdrew.

Abdullah laughed again, wiping a few drops of wine from his beard. "You English! Always so polite. It is a wonder you have such a great empire."

"Ah," I said hesitantly, "may I ask if my companion, Uuka, may have a meal. We have only dried meat with us."

He waved one greasy hand. "It has already been seen to, my friend. I shall care for your servant as I would any of mine. He has been fed and he may stay near your tent, if you wish."

"If it is all the same, I would prefer that he stay in the tent with me," I said.

He tilted his head and furrowed his brow, then nodded. "Of course, you wish to make certain he does not run away. Did others run off when the Portuguese thieves attacked?"

"Some did, yes," I admitted.

He nodded knowingly, as though he had expected as much.

As we finished the meal and I had eaten more than I have in one sitting in ages, though more out of politeness, his servants quietly removed plates and returned with bowls of fragrant water once more. One servant brought in a small tray with cigarettes, offering them to the prince, then to me.

Abdullah took one, which another servant lit from a taper.

I declined the offered cigarettes. "Would you mind?" I asked, pulling my pipe from the pocket of my jacket.

"Of course not! Indulge yourself. Now, tell me what brings you this far from your home and what these Portuguese stole from you."

Briefly I told him about their attack, the killing of my oxen, and being stuck underneath my wagon. I explained how, unarmed, Uuka had fled with other men, but had returned to pull me free. "They took my other wagon, which was driven by a faithful old Hottentot who has been with me since I was a boy, as well as some of our men."

"They will be sold on the coast," he said. "If they survive the march. If the old man is strong enough, there is hope for him, but I cannot see that he would be worth much to them to take all that distance."

"He's pretty clever," I said.

Abdullah humphed. "An intelligent slave is worth even less than a weak one. He will be fortunate they do not kill him out of hand. The Portuguese are known for their cruelty to their slaves. I believe I know the man who leads that expedition. Delgotto. He is an old rival of mine. He has stolen from me before, and I have stolen from him. I have heard from a village we passed that a hunter had killed some elephants, taking the ivory and giving them the meat. That was you, was it not?"

I admitted it was.

"I knew that it could not have been Delgotto who hunted the elephants," he said. "He would have left the meat to rot rather than give it to any of the locals, and taken half the village as slaves. So, he has taken your ivory. You see, I have been after that herd of elephants, too, my friend, and I suspect so has Delgotto. You were fortunate to find it first. Or perhaps unfortunate, since Delgotto went after you rather than the herd. It was easier for him to take the tusks from you than from the elephants. He is a better thief than he is a hunter, and he was in haste, probably because he has heard that I am in the area. He did not take the time to plunder your second wagon. You are fortunate that you were trapped underneath it or you would have been as dead as your oxen."

"He may not have found it as easy," I said.

He laughed. "Ah, you are as arrogant as any Englishman. What do you intend to do?"

"I intend to hunt down this Delgotto, or whoever it was who attacked us and took my men prisoner."

"You, with one servant?"

"If he will join me. Uuka can leave whenever he wants. I would not force him to follow me."

Abdullah frowned and shook his head. "Then you will bring about his death as well as your own. Delgotto has many men with him and many guns. Facing him would be suicide. Do you prize your ivory over your own life?"

"I don't care a fig about the ivory," I said, a bit sharply, although he took no offence. "I must rescue Hans and the other men. They are my responsibility."

"I have never heard of such devotion," he said.

"Hans has saved my life many times before," I said.

"Ah, a life debt I can understand. And responsibility, this too I understand, for I am a prince over many. But you will have no hope against so many foes."

I had to admit to myself that he was right; although there was some small chance Uuka and I could sneak up upon Delgotto's people and rescue our companions. I would never turn away from my course, but it seemed to be a doomed enterprise. A small glimmer of hope came to me as I looked at the Arab reclining before me.

"You are hunting for ivory, too, aren't you, Prince."

"I am."

"Then you would like to have the ivory Delgotto stole from me."

"To take a treasure without much work, that is desirable; however, Delgotto is a wily old pirate. He would not give up the treasure so easily, and I know he has more men than I. No, my friend, it would not be worth my involvement. I am sorry, but I cannot help you."

"If I paid you in ivory?" I asked.

"You must first win back your ivory, and that is the problem."

"But Delgotto did not steal all of my ivory," I said.

He stroked his beard for several minutes, then wagged his finger at me. "You had two wagons. Of course both would be loaded with tusks. But you realize that I could just follow your tracks and find the ivory you left behind."

"It's hidden," I said.

"Yes, you would take that precaution. So, how much ivory are we discussing?"

I told him.

He pursed his lips. "And Delgotto has taken the same amount?"

"Yes."

"That is quite a fortune," he said. "And if we speak hypothetically and we catch Delgotto and take this wagon full of tusks from him and his many armed men, how much is to be your take?"

"None," I said.

"You wish only to visit vengeance on Delgotto?"

"I wish only to rescue my men," I said. "If you are willing to help me pursue Delgotto, you may have the ivory that I have hidden. If we can find and defeat Delgotto, then you may have the rest. If possible, I would like my wagon back, but that is negotiable."

"And when will you pay me this hidden cache of ivory?"

"In the morning. Uuka can lead your men to it while I set off after Delgotto."

"And what would stop me from taking this ivory and going on my way?"

"Nothing," I said. "You may have it, if only in payment for you hospitality tonight. Although I know that you are an honorable man."

He sat back and puffed on his cigarette, smoke curling around his head.

"Indeed," he said after a while, "I am honorable and you are my guest. I will accept your ivory in payment for accompanying you in your pursuit of the accursed thief, Delgotto. He has been a stone under my saddle for many years. Besides, your ivory will help to shorten my trip. If I can take from this Portuguese what he has taken, so much the better."

He reached out his big hand and I took it, wondering what sort of deal I had struck.

When I returned to the tent that had been given to me for the night, I whispered to Uuka all that had transpired. He was less than enthusiastic.

"*Inkosi*," he said, "although I do not like the idea of only two of us hunting down these thieves and slavers, as the odds are not in our favor, I do not like this smiling Arab. He has some Arabs with him with old guns, and many servants, but I do not trust him. Arab slavers have taken black people for many, many years, long before the Portuguese or Dutch. They take our women for their harems; they cut our young men and make them eunuchs."

I knew that the Arab slave trade had gone on since the seventh century, and I had heard of the atrocities that still existed. I did not, however, see evidence of slaves among the people in Abdullah's camp. There were many servants who acted fearful, and perhaps they were slaves, but he did not appear to be transporting any captured blacks to be sold on the slave dockets. No one was bound or fettered. With the exception of the armed Arab escort, his retinue of blacks were bearers of supplies. From what I have seen, Abdullah was a merchant and trader. Until I was shown the contrary, I would take him at his word that he had been on the hunt for ivory, as I had been.

I tried to alleviate Uuka's fears, without success.

I told him that he would be leading some of Prince Abdullah's men back through the pass, to the cave where he had hidden the ivory. He was to give them all except the two tusks that he had buried.

"I hope that Hans appreciates what he is worth," Uuka mumbled as he tried to go to sleep near the tent's entrance, hugging his rifle.

At sunrise, Uuka reluctantly led three of Abdullah's Arabs and fifteen bearers back the way we had come, while the rest broke down camp and started after the trail of my stolen wagon. He would eventually join us, whereas those with the tusks would take their time in catching us up.

Abdullah rode his horse with its splendid trappings and his rich and colorful robes, while I kept pace on foot. I grew impatient, for the long line of his men and bearers trudged behind at what seemed to me a snail's pace. I wanted to rush ahead, or at least urge everyone on to greater speed, but any subtle remark went unnoticed. At any new rise, I expected to find Hans' body laying beside the tracks, having been murdered and tossed aside. He was a wiry old man, annoying and troublesome. He was bound to talk too much and obey too little, both excuses for a slave trader to be rid of him. I could not imagine any slaver considering Hans worth the effort to drag across the hills and grasslands to the coast, but I was grateful that I did not stumble upon his rotting carcass, so I clung to frail hope.

When evening came, Abdullah's tent was pitched, as was the smaller one for my use.

Uuka soon staggered in, along with one of the Arab escorts, who went to report to Abdullah. Uuka collapsed and I gave him some water, after which he related that all had gone as planned and that Abdullah's bearers were bringing along the tusks. Presently, the prince sent for me to join him again for dinner, and he seemed pleased.

"I have been told that your servant has taken my people to your hidden ivory," he said. "My bearers still march to catch up to us. I am told that the ivory is of good quality and will fetch quite a price. I will therefore fulfill my end of the bargain, Hunter Quatermain. We will hunt down these sons of pigs, these Portuguese. You have my word."

The next day, the trail we tracked joined the spoor of many people. There were signs of at least a hundred, and I wondered how we might fight against such a force. Prince Abdullah had only a dozen armed men, and those weapons ranged from muzzle loaders to scimitars. Uuka and I had Martini Henrys, and although modern for the time, they still took one cartridge at a time. We were a small force against many, but the prince seemed excited over the prospect of facing down his old enemy. Uuka, too, was concerned, but not so much over an impending conflict. He did not trust Abdullah and whispered his belief that the Arab prince would merely take the ivory, kill me in the night, and sell him into slavery.

"I do not worry for myself, Macumazahn," he insisted. "I am but a poor servant and am of no consequence. My life is small in the eyes of the Great-great. Whether I die tomorrow or am sold on the block, does not matter. But you will be dead, and that is a great loss."

"Nonsense," I said. "First of all, we are not going to die. Abdullah may be a scoundrel, but he has given his word and I believe that he is bound to it. As for you in the eyes of God, you are no less than me. God sees us as equal, Uuka. In the Bible, John 13, I believe, it says something like 'The servant is not greater than his lord; neither he that is sent greater than he that sent him.' So none of that unworthy nonsense. If you are worried, you may leave at any time. I keep telling you that. But I am bound to rescue Hans and the others. They are my responsibility, as you are. I will not force you to follow me in this endeavor."

He beamed at me in the lamp light. "The words of the Great-great say that we are equal? I would like to see more of His words, if only I could read."

So I dug out my battered Bible, squinted under the lamp, and read out loud until he fell asleep.

Upon the next day, we saw fresher signs of our quarry, indicating that we were closing upon them. Abdullah, seated upon his horse, observed the spoor I showed him and stroked his beard.

"Delgotto may have spies lingering behind," he said, "in case they might be followed. If I had stolen something of such wealth, as your ivory, I would do the same. He knows I am near, but does not know I am in pursuit. Still, he would leave someone just behind the main body, to watch for signs such as dust clouds or smoke from cooking fires, or fire glows at night. We must be more cautious, Hunter Quatermain, if we are to overtake them. We are gaining on them, because they are such a large group and move slower than us."

"Perhaps if only your armed men proceed with us," I suggested, "leaving all the bearers behind for now."

Stroking his beard again, he considered the suggestion.

"I must have men to guard the bearers," he said, "or they will run away with my property. If we camp here for a time, I may send a man ahead to determine how far we must yet march before we encounter Delgotto. If it will be soon, then we may take most of my men to attack, leaving the slower ones and the ones who cannot shoot straight with the camp."

"Uuka and I can go ahead," I suggested, "and observe from a distance. Then return with our report."

He looked at me steadily, as though he were calculating a deal which did not tend to favor him. "I think not, my friend. Although we have broke bread and I have given my hospitality, as well as my assistance, I could understand that a man might be tempted, no matter how righteous he might seem. You might find your wagon of ivory and sneak away with it, leaving poor Abdullah behind."

"The thought never crossed my mind," I said in earnest. My tone was sharp, for this accusation insulted me.

He waved his hand. "Of course, of course. But given the opportunity, your resolve might weaken, and then where would I be? You may go to spy on the Portuguese, but I insist that my man Hassim accompanies you. He is very trustworthy and silent of feet."

"Three of us would be more likely to be noticed," I said.

"Ah, but your servant shall remain with me. Do not worry. He shall be well taken care of, as though he were one of my own. I know you favor him, so you have incentive to return to me."

He smiled innocently, as though he had no intention of holding Uuka as a hostage but was merely protecting him, but his motives were clear, and he knew that I understood. Anger raged in me that my word should be challenged in such a manner, but I held my tongue. Should I start to argue with the prince, he could easily kill me and then go after the rest of the ivory on his own, leaving Hans and the others to their fate with the slavers.

I took a deep breath to calm my nerves, then bowed my head. "As you wish, Prince Abdullah. It is not necessary, but I am at your bidding."

Before I left with Hassim, Uuka whispered urgently to me.

"Please hurry back, Macumazahn. I do not like the looks of this Arab prince. He is just as likely to leave with what ivory he has taken from you and sell me in Zanzibar. I do not want to be a eunuch."

I assured him I would not be long, although Abdullah's behavior concerned me. Could I count on him to still be here when I returned? Of course, one of his men would be with me, and I doubted he would abandon both of us, particularly when there was more ivory to be had.

As Abdullah's servants began raising the tents and arranging their burdens, Hassim and I began our trek across the veldt.

The Arab was tall, wiry, and quiet. His dark features wore a perpetual brooding scowl. He carried an old jezail muzzle-loader with a long, curved stock of polished wood inlaid with ivory. I admired the workmanship and told him as much, inquiring if he had made it himself. He replied that it had been made by his father and given to him upon his father's death. Then he lapsed into silence. The curved sword sheathed at his side was decorated less ostentatiously, with fine designs and Arabic script etched into the metal scabbard and hilt. I had no desire to question him on its origin, afraid of some other tragic story. He was not one who instilled companionable dialogue, so I refrained from making conversation and concentrated on locating Delgotto's party.

Night fell before we grew close enough, fires throughout the camp alerting us to their presence. We crested one hill only to find them parked upon the next. White canvas tents perched on the top of the hill, and in their midst, illuminated by camp fires, was my wagon. I could not see the oxen, but I could hear an occasional snort coming from far off to the right. They were probably set out to graze, hobbled to prevent them from wandering too far away.

I could see movement among the tents, though it was too far and too dark to see clearly. There appeared to be a number of men in European clothes. Upon the slope of the hill, there was an occasional man walking among the prone or sitting figures resting or sleeping in small groups. These guards were also in European clothing and carried rifles. I would have liked to have my telescope, and I should have thought to ask Abdullah if he had any with him. As it was, I could only guess at how many armed men Delgotto had with him.

I decided to move closer in hopes that I might see Hans, maybe recognize that filthy old hat he always wore, but Hassim caught me by the arm.

"We go back now," he said.

"No," I said, "I want to get closer."

He shook his head. "No. We will be noticed."

Perhaps he would, for he moved with heavy feet through the grass. He was used to marches across the open country. I, however, have lived most of my life sneaking up on game. I could move almost silently, which is not bragging but merely stating a fact. It is part of my vocation, as an accountant can add numbers in his head more rapidly than the average person. But trying to explain this to a moody, unimaginative Arab was impossible.

I tried to impress upon him the importance of his remaining hidden behind an acacia tree while I moved down the slope to the right, but he had none of it. Perhaps he thought I was going to try to steal back my oxen. I have no idea. I certainly could not get my wagon away without the oxen, and I certainly could not round up the team by myself, let alone harness them without anyone in the camp knowing it, since the wagon itself was in the center of the camp. Hassim never bothered to explain his reasoning, but trudged after me.

With his tramping through the tall grass, trying to catch up with me, I decided to abandon my attempts at getting closer and turned to make a hasty retreat. However, this action came too late. One of the sentries had already turned his attention toward us. He shouted something I did not understand, which I can only assume was in Portuguese.

He was not one who instilled companionable dialogue...

Hassim's answer was to tuck the curve of his musket under his arm and fire.

Despite the distance, Hassim's bullet struck its mark and the Portuguese threw out his arms and fell over backwards.

Murmurs and shouts spilled through the camp.

"Run!" I shouted to Hassim.

I ran past him up the slope as gunfire thundered from the camp. He stood for a moment, then began to sprint past me. He was half my age and in fine condition. Although I can keep up a good pace, the leg that had been maimed by a lion some years before gave me trouble. I walk with a slight limp. Running can prove difficult. I made the crest of the hill, but only just ahead of the bullets that kicked up dirt and tore splinters from the acacia tree. By the time I pressed my back to the tree, Hassim had been swallowed up by the night.

Delgotto's men swarmed the hill.

I had three choices. I could make a stand and shoot a few of them before they overwhelmed me. I could surrender and hope they showed mercy. Or I could run. I chose the last action. Unfortunately, I was not swift, for the reason I have already stated. Nor did I consider the fact that they had horses. Two men on horseback came at me from the right, running me down. They could have easily shot me, but they seemed to want to capture me alive. One horse crashed into me, making me stumble, then the other shoved against me from the other side, and I went sprawling through the grass. I expected to be trampled, but the riders jumped from the bare backs of their mounts and tugged my rifle and my revolver away. One used my own Martini Henry to club me over the head.

Others came and dragged me to my feet. They bound my hands in front of me, then threw a noose around my neck. Now I wondered if they might use that acacia to throw the rope over a branch and hang me. Instead, the riders climbed onto their horses and one took the rope that went around my neck and pulled me along behind him. In case I needed more incentive to follow, the men on foot prodded me with their rifles and curses.

I followed behind the two horses, surrounded by a half dozen men, all shouting in Portuguese. They went down the hill, across a dry steam bed, then up the next incline. A path was made for us by the people who had been lying or sitting upon the ground. They rose up and quickly made way, and as they did so, I heard the rattling of metal chains. In the fog of my battered brain, I looked past my tormentors to these unfortunate souls. An occasional young man, but mostly women, with young girls and some boys, chains between manacled wrists and iron collars. From gaunt faces, their hollow eyes glanced at me with emptiness, if they looked up at all. Most of them just stared at the ground as they scurried out of the way.

I stumbled when I saw all of these naked, bruised and battered bodies around me, but trudged on when a rifle butt jabbed into my side.

They dropped me in the center of their camp on the hilltop, next to my own wagon, surrounded by three canvass tents. When the horseman released his grip on the rope that pulled me along and rode off with his companion, I dropped to my knees, my wounded head aching, the world spinning around me.

Someone kicked my already bruised side, and I fell against the forward wheel of the wagon. Looking up, I saw a stocky man standing over me, hands on hips, eyes glaring red with the reflection of the nearby fire. He was dressed in a white linen suit that had seen better days, a wide brimmed hat pushed back over his black curly hair. The trimmed beard was streaked with white.

One of his men held out my revolver, which he examined before shoving into his belt. Another man held out my Martini Henry, whereupon he nodded and spat at it.

"This is what killed Philippe," he said in a thick accent.

"Wasn't me," I managed to say. My words were a bit slurred, but at least the camp was no longer spinning around me.

"Liar!" He spat again, into the dirt at my feet. He leaned over and glared at me in rage. I met his stare with my own.

"It was an Arab that killed your man," I said. "Check my rifle. It hasn't been fired."

He scowled at me, but then straightened and snapped his finger to one of his men. My rifle was handed over, and he ran his finger over the barrel, then lifted it to his nose and sniffed at the breach. He grunted, then handed the weapon off.

"Who are you?" he demanded.

"Allan Quatermain."

"What do you want, coming here at night? And with an Arab, as you say."

"I'm a hunter. I saw your camp from a distance and came to look at it out of curiosity. The Arab was startled and shot when he had no reason."

"An Arab," he said, thoughtfully. "And are there more Arabs? I have rivals among them, and I believe one has been at my heels, preparing to swoop down and steal what is mine. So, where are these Arabs?"

"Only the one was with me," I said truthfully.

He shook his head, then wagged his finger at me. "There is more to you, hunter, than you let on."

He called one of his men to him, spoke in rapid Portuguese, and the man hurried away. Delgotto, for I assumed that was who faced me, paced in front of me with an expression of deep thought, eyeing me as though I were a puzzle to solve.

Presently, two men pushed their way through the crowd that had gathered around us and shoved a squirming figure into our midst.

"Ah Baas! You have found me! Alas, it seems we shall die together. I have failed your father the Predikant. I had sworn to take care of you, but you have come to find poor Hans and will share his fate, or worse."

"Hans," I said evenly, "be quiet."

The old Hottentot wore manacles on his thin wrists but no metal collar. He still had his battered hat, perched on the back of his graying head.

"I thought as much," Delgotto said. "You are the man this black has been babbling about all this time. Macumazahn, he called you. Macumazahn would come for him. Macumazahn would rescue him. He talked so much I was going to shoot him myself several times, but he insisted he was worth lots of money. I personally doubt he will make it to the coast. I told myself that if he survives that long, then I will see if he is worth anything. But his incessant chatter is worse than old women and he is very close to having one of my bullets to chew on."

"But you see," Hans said, "I told you "

Delgotto pulled my revolver from his belt and swung it toward Hans, who covered his head with his arms, rattling his chains.

"You see?" Delgotto declared to me. "He is worse than an old woman."

"He has always been that way," I said.

He used the gun to wave it at the wagon at my back.

"And this was yours? My men took your wagon. We heard about the great hunter from a village we raided and I sent men to see if they could find you. But my men, *estúpido*! They kill your oxen and make your wagon wreck. They thought you were dead and left the wagon and whatever it carried. And they brought me this old man, with monkeys in his head. What am I to do with him? Tell me, Hunter, did the other wagon have ivory, also?"

"Yes," I said.

Delgotto scowled. "I should kill them for leaving it."

Some of the men around him scattered, disappearing into the gloom.

He came close to me, waving my revolver in my face. "Where is it now?

Where is the other load of ivory? Did you fix the wagon? Did you bring it with you?"

"No," I said. "The wagon was wrecked. Even if I could have fixed it by myself, my oxen were dead."

"And the ivory? Where is it?"

"Still there. I couldn't very well carry it by myself."

"You weren't alone, though. You had blacks who ran away. Did you have this Arab with you? Who is he?"

"My men ran away when your people attacked. I came across the Arab when I was hunting you down."

"The great hunter was hunting me? So you could get your ivory back?"

"So I could get Hans back. I don't like to do my own cooking."

Delgotto stared at me for a moment, then leaned back and laughed. After he recovered, he gave a wide smile with crooked yellow teeth, what few he had. "You, you are clever. I think I like you, Hunter. I will feel very bad when I have to kill you."

"Image how I'll feel," I said.

He laughed again. "Well, we keep you around a little while. We torture you some, to find out about this Arab who killed Philippe. He needs to answer for this murder. You, you will pay for your part. Oh, I know that you did not shoot, but you led the Arab here, so you are responsible. But first, you will answer questions. Then we execute you. So tell me, Englishman, where is this murdering Arab?"

"He ran away," I said.

"Where are the other Arabs? I know there are others. I have heard of an Arab trader in the territory. Where is he?"

"The Arab who was with me was alone. He was lost from his companions."

"But you were tracking me? Why? You want your ivory."

"I came after Hans. You can keep the ivory."

Delgotto laughed. "Oh. I intend to. But why would you risk your life for this old woman of a man? He is worth nothing. I don't even know why my men brought him back with the wagon. They captured three others, who are young and strong. But this shriveled old thing … I gave my word that if he lived through the trip, he would be sold, but he would probably pay me less than the food he has eaten. Very well, if you prize him so highly, perhaps you will tell me more about the Arab in order to save his worthless life."

He pointed my revolver at Hans' head and cocked the hammer.

Hans covered his head again and began praying.

"Is he worth more ivory?" I asked.

Delgotto glared at me. "What ivory?"

"The tusks your men left in my second wagon. It's all still there. Send this wagon back, and you can have twice as much as this one load."

He scowled. "I can have that anyway. There is nothing stopping me from sending my men back for it."

"But they won't find it if it is hidden," I said.

"So you hid the ivory? Then you will tell me where it is."

"Let Hans and my three other men go," I said, "and I will take you to the ivory."

He lifted the gun, pointing it to the sky, and thought for a time. Then he shook his head. "I do not think so."

Hans groveled upon the ground. "Don't give him the gold, Baas!"

"Gold?" Delgotto said suddenly. "What gold?"

I almost asked Hans the same question, but just stared dumbly at him.

"Do not tell him about the gold," Hans said.

They must have beat him, particularly in the head, for he was now talking nonsense. Of course we had no gold. I had not tried my hand at prospecting for many years, and it was possible that Hans' poor brain was so befuddled that he had regressed to that earlier time out of confusion. There was no other explanation for his claim that we had gold, which was adding another dangerous element to our already precarious position.

Delgotto kicked the cowering Hottentot. "What gold!"

"Ooh! Sorry Baas. He knows about your gold." Hans began babbling.

Delgotto grabbed him by the chains welded to the manacles encircling his wrists and shook them, rattling his old bones.

"Tell me about the gold, you old fool! How much gold? Where is it?"

"He's lying," I said. "He's been hit on the head too many times."

Delgotto glared over his shoulder at me. "You be quiet!" Then he shook Hans again. "Tell me!"

"Bags of gold," he said. "In the other wagon. Oh, Baas, I am sorry. He beat it out of me."

"Idiot," I said.

Delgotto shoved Hans to the ground and turned on me. "So, you offer me ivory, when you have bags of gold hidden away. Well, Hunter, you will take me there and give me both the gold and the ivory, or I shall leave your rotting corpse on this hill."

I had no doubt that had been his intention all along.

"But the Baas is the only one who knows where they are," Hans said.

"Then I shall kill you," Delgotto said, training the weapon on Hans once more.

Hans shrugged. "Then if I save the Baas once more, I have done good."

"Hold it!" I snapped. "He's lying about gold. I'll take you to the ivory, but there is no gold."

Delgotto stood up and contemplated us both. After a time, he said, "Normally, I would not believe a black no matter what he says, but I trust an Englishman even less. Jorge will take you back to your wagon, while we continue on. The two of you will take horses. You will give Jorge the gold, and he will let you live. If you do not give him the gold, or if as you say there is no gold, he will bring back your head in a sack. Jorge!"

A large man stepped into the firelight. He wore a ragged shirt with the sleeves torn off and carried a curved Arab dagger. He ran his thumb over the blade and grinned with a few crooked teeth.

"What about Hans?" I asked as they dragged me to my feet.

"You are in no position to bargain," Delgotto said. "I should just kill both of you now and save myself the trouble. But if there is a chance for gold, I shall take it. And I am feeling generous. If Jorge brings back gold rather than your head, then I will be magnanimous and set your old servant free. If Jorge brings back your head, then the old man will suffer for many days before he dies. It will be his reward for lying to me."

Hans glanced up at the Portuguese leader with his eyes wide and mouth slack. For once he was speechless.

Horses were brought, and I was lifted into the saddle of one. Jorge climbed onto the other, took the reins of my mount, and started off.

The sun was starting to rise over the hills and the men were beginning to make preparations for breaking camp. Those not shackled were forced to work on tearing down the tents, packing up supplies, and bearing them on the long march. My oxen were rounded up and hitched to my wagon. The people in chains were whipped to their feet while Delgotto and his fellows enjoyed a breakfast before mounting horses.

Trailing behind Jorge, I looked down upon the feeble prisoners beginning to stir. They were so pitiful that my heart broke. Previously, I had only seen them in the dark. I had no such advantage this time. Their agony was plane on their faces, as were the scars and fresh wounds they bore. None of them, even the children, had no illusions as to their fate. Their eyes showed souls already dead, lost in hopelessness. They did not even try to seek hope in me, as I was a prisoner myself and in no position to help. Furthermore, I was white. I was the same color as their tormentors.

I had some faint hope, as I was still alive and now only under the watchful eye of one man who thought he had great advantage over my smaller stature. To him I was a weak Englishman, but I could eventually turn the tables on him. He seemed savage, ready to slit my throat at the slightest provocation, but he was not very intelligent. My problem was returning to rescue Hans once I was able to overpower Jorge. I had no illusion that Prince Abdullah would still be willing to help. Hassim had vanished, probably returning to Abdullah's camp, and they were on their merry way to their own destination, with half of my ivory. When I freed myself of this present situation, I would be alone and relatively unarmed, a worse predicament than when I had started.

The morning dragged on as we trudged across the grassy hills.

I formed plans and discarded them. At some point we would need to rest, and then I would make my move, but I was not certain how I was to surprise and subdue the big Portuguese. He had only the long curved dagger and a musket strapped to his saddle. He could not easily shoot me, but he seemed quite capable of drawing that dagger in an instant and gutting me should I show any sign of treachery.

A cluster of acacia trees stood upon a hilltop, providing excellent shade from the mid-morning sun. I imagined Jorge would stop there for a rest, and then I would act, but to my surprise and disappointment, he guided the horses to pass the trees and not take sanctuary beneath them. We headed to the left of them, cresting the hill.

A terrible scream startled me, as well as the two horses.

From behind the acacia, another horse pounded into view and charged down upon us. Atop the beast, in a swirl of colorful robes, rode a savage of terrifying dimensions. This demon brandished a scimitar that cut through the air with a sound that rivaled the thunder of the hoof beats.

Jorge drew his dagger. He had no time to do anything else before the attacker was upon him.

The scimitar swung in a sweeping arc that sliced through the neck of the Portuguese.

In a heartbeat, the ferocious rider was past us. Jorge's head dropped one way from his shoulders and his body slid from his horse the other way. Now riderless, his horse bolted over the hill, dragging the headless corpse by one foot still stuck in a stirrup. My own horse, frightened by the attack, turned in the other direction and galloped away blindly. I could not grab the reins, with my hands bound, but could only hold onto the saddle and hope not to be thrown.

Before I realized it, the robed figure rode up and grabbed hold of the bridle, slowing my raging horse and bringing it to a halt.

"Ah, friend Quatermain!" Prince Abdullah said, grinning. "You seem to have run into difficulty."

His sword was now sheathed, so he drew a dagger and slit my bonds.

"Thank you," I said. "I seem to owe you yet again."

"It was a pleasure, my friend, to part that accursed Portuguese from his head. Were it only Delgotto instead of one of his underlings, then I would be in Paradise. But alas, that will soon be. Come, we will join the others and you shall tell me what has happened."

"How is it you are out here, Prince Abdullah?" I asked.

"Ah, well, I have my own spies. When Hassim returned and said that you had been captured, I decided to form a party to raid these Portuguese devils. One of my men I sent ahead, to watch our path. He saw you in the company of that headless one and returned to me to report. We waited among those trees, believing that you would seek the shade, but your captor had other plans. I could not very well allow my dear friend to be taken away, so I attacked."

I took up my reins and followed him to the cluster of trees, where his men made themselves known. One led Jorge's horse, minus the dead rider. However, I did notice the dagger of the late Portuguese sticking in the sash of this particular Arab.

One man among the group ran forward, a grin on his dark face.

"Macumazahn!"

Uuka, with the other Martini Henry slung over his shoulder, hurried up to my horse. "You are alive. And free! Praise the Great-great." Then he glanced surreptitiously at the Arabs after his outburst.

Some of the Arabs glared at him, though I suspected most did not understand his English. Abdullah ignored him.

"Your servant insisted on coming to your rescue," Abdullah said. "I saw no harm in it, especially since he would be better with your fancy rifle than any of my men. The more the better in fighting these thieving Portuguese. And I could always kill him later." Then he laughed.

Uuka did not find the remark amusing, but hid himself on the other side of my horse.

"So," Abdullah said, "what is your plan, Hunter Quatermain?"

I looked around at the ten Arabs armed with swords and either jezail or Kabyle muskets. Delgotto had more men, although I did not see how most of them were armed. I still could not see how we would overcome

"Come, we will join the others and you shall tell me what has happened."

the more numerous Portuguese, who also employed blacks among their armed contingent. They moved slower as a group because of their slave captives, but that could also cause difficulty, as they could use the prisoners as shields.

"We could move ahead of them," I suggested, "and set up an ambush. However, I do not know the terrain. There may not be a place to bottleneck them."

Abdullah shook his head. "I too am unfamiliar with this territory. If the hills are too far apart, we may not be able to get close enough to shoot accurately, and we must work with the element of surprise on our side, since we are outnumbered."

"Then perhaps your swords would be the best weapons," I said. "And night our camouflage."

Abdullah grinned. "We shall haunt them until they rest for the night. Then we shall strike like ghosts and spirit away their souls. Brilliant!"

I was still not convinced that our small group would overcome the Portuguese.

Despite my misgivings, Abdullah assigned Hassim to sneak ahead and watch the Delgotto party from a distance. At least he left his rifle behind, which would preclude him from shooting another one of Delgotto's men. The prince had given him Jorge's horse, so that he might more swiftly return, or flee if he was spotted. And should he either be captured or the horse he rode be recognized as belonging to the ill-fated Portuguese, I expected Hans' life would be forfeit. However, I had no say in the matter, even though I politely voiced my opinion. Although Abdullah had the ivory to gain, he seemed singularly obsessed with overtaking and overcoming the Portuguese, as though it were a matter of honor.

Hassim returned at dusk to inform us that Delgotto had set up camp on a grassy plain. There were no hills to skulk behind, no trees for concealment. The only fires that were lit were in the center of the camp, among the tents and wagon. The captured slaves were fed some gruel, then forced to bed on the cold ground in a circle around the camp, watched over by armed sentries who wandered the perimeter.

As a group, we crept towards the camp, then Abdullah sent his men to spread out, encircling the area. I expected an alarm to arise at any moment, as these Arabs were not stealthy. However, the Portuguese sentries and the blacks the Portuguese employ must have been oblivious to any sounds beyond their camp, for the Arabs approached unnoticed. The occasional stirring of their captives and the rattling of chains did wonders to hide the approach of Abdullah's assassins. When the opportunity arose, they did indeed swoop in like ghosts, as I witnessed. One large black sentry, his ebony skin covered in ritual scars, passed between us and the camp. From the deep grass, a swirl of white robes rose into the air and engulfed the man. In a moment his throat was sliced open and he was lowered quietly to the ground to gasp his last breath.

In the darkness, other sentries fell under similar attacks. I do not know how well these Arabs hunted game, but they were efficient hunters of men.

I followed Abdullah through the path between clusters of human flesh. The captured slaves stirred at our approach, murmuring and clinking chains. I whispered in various Bantu dialects that they remain quiet and still, that I was there to help them. I imagined that these poor creatures were taken from nearby villages, like the one that had aided me in the elephant hunt. I wondered if any of these people had seen me then and remembered me. But some were so thin and frail, they had to have come from even further away, forced to endure these hardships or die along the way to the coast. If all went as planned, they would soon be released and on their long journey home. But first our small force must defeat the Portuguese, a feat that could fail if these people caused enough noise to disturb the camp.

But the mutterings continued.

Fear must have spread among the captives at the sight of the Arabs, for the sounds of women crying came from one side of the camp.

One of Delgotto's men ducked out of his tent, rifle in hand, and squinted into the dark surrounding the camp. He spoke in low tones, bringing out three more men.

This first one called out. I could not catch what he said, but it may have been a name of one of the sentries. Since no one made a reply, I assumed that guard now lay in the dirt with a sliced throat. So he called out again, with a different name, and again received no reply.

He and his fellows immediately became agitated and roused others in the other tents.

A rifle blast through the stillness, like thunder on a clear evening.

One of the Portuguese threw out his arms and fell onto the ground.

Now the shouts came, as well as screams from the frightened captives. Shots rang out, muzzle fire flaring in the dark all around the camp.

Delgotto stormed from his tent, firing my revolver.

The other men shot into the dark, unconcerned whether they hit innocent slaves or the attackers. Delgotto kicked dirt onto the fire next to him, plunging his tents into darkness. He and his men became shadows moving in the night, crouching near my wagon for cover, shooting at whatever moved.

"This is not good," Abdullah said next to me.

We knelt on the trampled grass, ducking down to avoid the bullets of Delgotto's men. Around us, the captives hugged the ground, most whimpering in terror, the children clinging to whatever adult they were near.

"We must attack," I said, not adding that we must do so before Delgotto killed his own prisoners in an attempt to ward us off.

"Yes, we must," Abdullah said, immediately standing.

He unsheathed his sword and let loose a piercing war cry that chilled me to the bones. It was a terrible sound, like some banshee or demon from hell. Those captives around us seemed to cling closer to the ground, their own whimpering cries silenced in utter terror.

For a moment, the gunfire ceased. The cry emitted by the Arab prince echoed through the darkness and was taken up by each and every Arab surrounding the camp.

Delgotto and his dozen or so men froze.

Then Abdullah charged, a flurry of robes running toward the center of the camp.

In the gloom I could see others to my right and left as they too attacked, robes flowing ghostlike in what little light the dying embers of the camp fires provided.

Gun shots continued, but Delgotto's men did not seem to hit any of their targets. Perhaps they were too shaken by the savage attack, or I just was unable to see any of the Arabs fall under the bullet, but Abdullah and his men converged on the center of the camp in a barbaric onslaught that rivaled any ancient battle scene.

Scimitars and daggers sliced through the air and human flesh with the same ease. In the flash of gunfire I was able to see some of the horrendous action as the Portuguese were butchered.

Uuka hunkered down next to me.

"Macumazahn," he said, "these Arabs are demons. We should flee."

"Find Hans and the other men," I told him. "Either release them or get them away somehow."

I did not wait to hear his reply, but ran ahead, clutching my Martini Henry and unable to distinguish a target in the darkness.

When I reached the middle of the camp, a faint light grew over the distant horizon, heralding the coming dawn. Two of the tents had been torn down; ropes hacked through by swinging swords. Half of Delgotto's men lay scattered over the ground, cut to pieces, dismembered and even decapitated. Two Arabs lay dead.

Unable to reload their weapons, the Portuguese each grabbed their muskets by the barrels and swung them like clubs, which were pitiful weapons against the Arab blades.

One of the blacks under Delgotto's command snatched up a scimitar from a fallen Arab and ran at the back of Prince Abdullah, with the apparent intent of parting his royal head from his shoulders.

I raised my rifle and fired.

The shots tore into his chest and through his heart. He stumbled and skid across the ground, sword falling from lifeless fingers, coming to rest at the heels of the prince.

Abdullah slashed his own advisory before he turned to notice the dead man at his back. He glanced at me with a wide grin and gave me a nod before turning back to plunge his sword into his opponent's chest.

"Where is Delgotto!" Abdullah shouted, lifting his bloody sword into the air.

The last of the Portuguese slavers dropped to his knees before Hassim, the Arab's sword driven through him, protruding out his back, but he still clung to life. Hassim tugged on his sword, pushing the man back with his foot. Once his blade was free, he swung wide and sliced through the man's neck. The look of terror remained on the face of his severed head as it rolled on the ground. His headless body toppled over a moment later.

Abdullah kicked one of the bodies over.

"Where is Delgotto?" he demanded again.

He tramped through the carnage, looking at each of the dead and mutilated white men.

A sound near the back of my wagon caught my attention, a scuffle and a rattle of chain. Turning, I saw Delgotto, shirt torn and bloody from numerous cuts, but none that appeared life threatening. He had one arm around the neck of Hans, holding him as a shield in front of him. In his other hand was my revolver, the barrel pressed against Hans' gray temple.

"Ah Baas," Hans said, his voice strained with the constriction from Delgotto's choking hold, "do not trouble yourself over me. I have lived a good life. Well, maybe not all good. But at least God forgives me."

"Shut up, you old fool!" Delgotto hissed, shaking Hans, strangling him.

"It's finished, Delgotto," I said. "Let him go, and you can ride away."

The man laughed, nodding toward Abdullah. "Do you expect me to believe that he will allow me to live? You surprise me, Quatermain. I never would have expected you to be in league with the likes of Prince Abdullah."

"We are brothers, he and I," Abdullah said. "The Hunter and I are of one blood."

"I find that hard to believe," Delgotto said. "Quatermain, you prize the life of this old black. You risked your life for his rescue. And for the others who were taken with him. Yet you are in the company of the likes of Abdullah."

"He's helped me hunt you down," I said, wondering how I might convince him to lower the revolver and release Hans.

"You think me a devil, Quatermain," Delgotto said, "because I deal in slaves. What do you know of Abdullah."

"He's a merchant and trader," I said. "I promised him the ivory you stole from me if he would help me."

"Merchant and trader, yes," the Portuguese said. "But in what commodities? Are you that dim that you do not know his main revenue? Do you think he helped hunt me down merely for your ivory?"

"Of course," I said.

"Then you are very naïve," he said. "Or blinded by your own desire to rescue this old fool. You think I am a greater merchant in flesh? I am nothing compared to Prince Abdullah, whose fame has spread all along the east coast of Africa. He didn't come after me for your ivory, although I am certain he will put that to good use, but to take my captives."

"No," I said. "All of those people will be released and I'll see that they return to their homes. Let Hans go and I will assure you that you can leave here unmolested."

"No," he said. "I will not be leaving here."

For a brief moment I saw the hopelessness in his eyes. He had us at a stalemate by holding Hans as a shield, but he knew that he had little time left. Had he surrendered, I had little doubt that I could convince Abdullah to allow him his freedom, since he was alone and now outnumbered. But he could not see Abdullah granting mercy. He turned his gun toward us, whether to me or to Abdullah, I could not tell. I could not give him the opportunity to fire first. Now that the weapon was no longer pressed to Hans' temple, I raised my rifle.

With only a split second to aim, I fired,

The back of Delgotto's head exploded, and he crumpled to the ground.

The Arabs around the camp began cheering and warbling, dancing about, rifles and swords swaying in the air.

Hans sagged and began to breathe as though he had held his breath during the entire ordeal.

"Very good shot, my friend!" Abdullah declared.

Shouldering my rifle, I ran to Hans, then knelt and searched Delgotto's body. As I suspected, he had a master key to the manacles. I picked up my fallen pistol and shoved it into its holster, then, using the key, I released Hans from his chains.

"I knew you would save me, Baas. I prayed you would come back and rescue old Hans. The lie I told about the gold was so that you could get away and escape; then come back for me."

"Just be quiet and listen," I said, pressing the key into his palm. "Uuka is searching for the other men who were captured with you. Find him, then start releasing all of the slaves."

"That will not be a very good idea," Abdullah said as he approached us.

I motioned to my wagon next to us. "The ivory is there. It's all yours, just as we agreed."

"And you have your servant," Abdullah said as he wiped his sword clean on a rag torn form a dead man's shirt. "Your other man will find the others you sought, and they may be released, as was our bargain. You may even have your wagon. But that is all."

I stepped closer to him. "I don't intend to take any of these people. I just want them released."

He slipped his scimitar into its scabbard and waved one hand toward the wagon. "But I have all this ivory. I must have bearers to carry it all the way north."

"These people were captured to be slaves," I insisted. "They must be released."

Abdullah grinned and shook his head. "That was not part of our bargain. If you want them released, you must pay me many more tusks."

"I don't have any more ivory."

He lifted his arms. "Then we cannot make any further deals. Take your wagon and oxen, and your five blacks. That is what we agreed upon. The rest are mine."

"Then what Delgotto said is true," I said, anger rising. "You're a slaver too."

"Of course, my friend. I have never denied it. I have even told you that Delgotto and I were rivals. What did you think? That we tried to outdo each other in the trade of jewelry and ivory? Sometimes he would steal my captives, and sometimes I would steal his. He has been a thorn in my side for many years, raiding villages before I would arrive, stealing from me, leaving me only the weak to take. Now you have removed that thorn, my friend. I am grateful."

"Grateful enough to let these people go?" I asked.

He laughed, as though I had made a great joke.

I drew my revolver and aimed it at him.

The Arabs who were looting the camp supplies turned angry faces toward me. Hassim lifted a rifle in my direction. Others placed hands on the hilts of swords and daggers.

"If you do not release every one of the prisoners," I said evenly, controlling my rage, "I will kill you."

Abdullah shook his head sadly. "My dear friend, you will not shoot me. You will do as we have agreed. You see, if you kill me, you too will die, and this old servant of yours, as well. And Uuka and your other men will be taken with all the other slaves. So, will you save this one's life and the others from slavery, or will you condemn all."

"I cannot let you take these people," I said. I clenched my teeth. My hand shook so much from my anger that I even doubted I could fire a killing shot, even at this distance.

Yet, I could not allow these people to be carted off to the slave block. The men to be forced into labor, the boys to be castrated, the girls and women to be mere objects of passion. Many would die along the way to their final destination among the Arab countries to the north and into India. For several hundreds of years this trade had been going on, and would probably continue for many more. What could I do against it? Sacrifice my life by killing one trader among so many others? Killing Abdullah would not release one person, and in fact condemn Uuka and the others. I had come to think of Abdullah as a friend, until I saw him as he truly was. He was charismatic and, I hated to admit it, likeable. Could I even put a bullet in him, after what we have endured together?

I lowered the hammer of my revolver and slipped it into its holster.

"Ah, Hunter Quatermain, my friend!" he shouted, grinning wide through his beard. "That is how friends should be. We both honor our word. Find your men and hook up your oxen, and I shall supply you for your journey. And I shall gather up my spoils and return home, thankful that we will never have to deal with the wretched Delgotto again. Songs will be sung of this day, my friend."

"I do not agree with what you do, Abdullah," I said, deflated, feeling as though I had suffered a great defeat. "And I will do whatever I can to put a stop to it."

"But not today, eh? We call a truce, shall we? You and I, unlikely friends and comrades. This has been a great victory for both of us. Let us savor that, my friend, and part on good terms, for when we meet again, we may be enemies. I pray to Allah that we will not, for I like you, Hunter Quatermain. You are a good and compassionate man."

I insisted that he keep my wagon and oxen. This surprised him, as my journey would be a long one, but I explained that I could not allow him to force his prisoners to bear the tusks on his even longer journey. The wagon might carry all of the tusks, once he met with the rest of his people. In return, he gave me three of Delgotto's horses, along with supplies. We would make our way back to the pass through the mountains where we would recovered the two remaining tusks Uuka had hidden, before returning to Natal.

I could not bear to look upon the faces of his captives as we left the encampment. They looked up at me, silently pleading, despair written on every one of them. I left them condemned to an awful life, and I doubted many would survive long. That I had saved Hans and the others was small consolation and did nothing to assuage my guilt at leaving those poor souls behind. Those faces, especially the young ones, haunted me for decades. Even as I write this, in my study in Yorkshire, I can see them as clearly as on that day. They haunt me still.

THE END

THE MAKING OF AN UNHOLY ALLIANCE

When I asked Ron Fortier how one submits to Airship 27, he presented me with a list of Public Domain characters from which to choose. The name Allan Quatermain immediately jumped out at me. Quatermain has been a hero since my youth, when I watched Stewart Granger in the 1950 version of *King Solomon's Mines* on TV with my father. Later, I read that book and was delighted to find others in the series and similar adventures by H. Rider Haggard. Quatermain was the epitome of the adventure hero, the precursor of characters like Indiana Jones, but the original character as written by Haggard was not quite what would be expected from most heroes. Small in stature, in his fifties by the time of King Solomon's Mines, walking with a limp, the son of a missionary, a student of the Bible, but he had an unerring sense of what was right.

Choosing this character led to two novels for Airship 27, and subsequently this short story for this anthology. My first novel was pure adventure, with some elements of science fiction thrown in for flavor. The second novel was fantasy, taking advantage of several African legends. Some legends, after all, begin with a grain of truth. For the present story, I wanted something different, as the original Quatermain stories tended to run the gambit of adventure to fantasy to historical drama. I decided to try something a bit more historical in nature, although none of my characters were actual historical figures.

The one trait of Quatermain's character that stands out for me above all others is his compassion. Despite uninformed accusations of racism, Quatermain's love for the African people is conspicuous, whether it is the tears he shed at the death of a long-time friend and companion or the memory of the beautiful Mameena that haunted him through several stories. How would he react to his servant and friend being taken by slavers?

While reading the histories of the early explorers of Africa, who would have been contemporaries with Quatermain, I had become fascinated by their friendship with a certain man, Tippu Tip, a slave trader from Zanzibar. This rather charismatic figure had befriended and aided both David Livingstone and Henry Stanley in their explorations of the interior, and without him they both would have perished. For my story, I created a fictional character loosely based on Tippu Tip. I wanted to see how Quatermain would react to such a person. Would he overlook this man's trading in human flesh for the sake of his own mission? Somehow, I felt Quatermain would behave differently than the great explorers.

In the three hundred years of the transatlantic slave trade, approximately eleven million Africans were transported across the Atlantic. 95% went to Central and South America, only 5% going to the United States. However, the Arab slave trade lasted over fourteen centuries, and in some areas still exists to this day. It is estimated that 150 million Africans were enslaved by Muslims, with an additional 50 million from other parts of the world. Very little attention is given to the Arab trade. As atrocious as slavery was in the United States, it was even worse elsewhere. Whereas there was a ten percent mortality rate for the Transatlantic trade, 80 to 90% of the captive slaves died in the East African and Transsahara trade. Men and young boys were castrated to prevent them from reproducing, many bleeding to death after the procedure. Children born to the women were often killed. Slaves in the Americas were allowed families, whereas those in the Middle East were not. More women were captured than men for the express purpose of sex slaves. As terrible as slavery has been, and still is, the whole story is not always told. In my present story, I can only scratch the surface.

Quatermain would have been aware of the slave trade in different parts of Africa, and if some of his men were taken, he would know how slim their chances of survival would be, and if they were fortunate to live through the transit, they were doomed to a short life of hard labor. Would he make a deal with one slaver to win his people from other slavers? Somehow, I could not see this happening. Had he known that Abdullah was primarily a slave trader, he would have struck out on his own, and more than likely failed. Abdullah never admitted to dealing in slaves until later. A type of myopia affected Quatermain, similar to that which afflicts him when dealing with the supernatural. He either ignores it or denies it in favor of his own world view. In this situation, he was so set on rescuing Hans he overlooked any sign that Abdullah was a slaver, despite Uuka's warnings. In the final scenes, he could not bring himself to commit murder, even though he believed Abdullah deserved it for the atrocity of slave trading. Leaving all those poor people to be dragged off and sold in Zanzibar tore him apart, but he had no choice. To him, he made a deal with the devil himself and he would never be free of the consequences. Such is the compassion of Allan Quatermain.

WAYNE CAREY – A life-long fan of science fiction and pulp fiction, Wayne Carey grew up reading Edgar Rice Burroughs, H.G. Wells, Isaac Asimov, H. Rider Haggard and all the grand masters, which guided him toward a career in science with degrees in biology and education and provided the desire to write from an early age. A love of classic and noire films, such as *Casablanca* and *The Maltese Falcon*, also influences his writing. He is the author of *The Nanon Factor*, a young adult contemporary science fiction thriller that blends a murder mystery with cutting edge technology, Airship 27's Quatermain: the New Adventures Volume 3, The Beast Men, and Volume 4, The Lightning Bird, and the supernatural thriller Company of Shadows, also from Airship 27, and has appeared in a variety of anthologies such as *Legends of New Pulp Fiction*. He and his wife Brenda live in the wilds of Central Pennsylvania with their three children, who provide a great deal of inspiration for his work. Email him at wgcarey@ProtonMail.com .

THE STAR OF WONDER

BY THOMAS KENT MILLER

There was the time in 1873, deciding to follow the advice of John Arkle, a man who was central to a story irrelevant to the one I, Allan Quatermain, am about to tell, as to the direction of travel when leaving the country of the Dabanda and the Holy Lake of Mone in Central Africa, I, with Hans, my old native companion and aide-de-camp since childhood and for my father before me, turned west with the intention of reaching the coast around Sierra Leone and locating an expedient ship or some such with which to return to South Africa and Durban, our home.

That journey took more months than I care to recall and can be divided into two distinct chapters. There was the actual trek between the country of the Holy Lake and the southeastern region of Sierra Leone contiguous with Liberia, a journey full of incident both good and bad, but totally separate from the subject of this tale. And then there were our experiences on the coast.

As we headed out of that amorphous and still largely unexplored region that we call for convenience Central Africa or Darkest Africa, despite my own journeys which in toto covered very little ground when considered geographically, we began to hear rumors from the various villages and occasional safari of a tribe of great white witch doctors and of the peculiar magic they wielded that required the building of a railroad for transport. When I asked what it was that was being transported, I received no clear answer but eventually concluded that it consisted of some sort of heavy equipment.

And since it was our encounter with those so-called white witch doctors, which description, by the way, could not be further from the truth, I will skip the fairly routine matters of signing papers, greasing palms, and stating intentions to officials, and get to the root of the episode.

With our retinue of wagons, oxen, and bearers, Hans and I entered the port community of Freetown, which was then in 1873 a growing hub of trading, with the aim of booking passage on the first vessel heading south. At this point we sold the wagons and oxen and dismissed the bearers and sold the various goods we'd accumulated on our trek from the various peoples we'd encountered.

That left only Hans and myself in this foreign land, as certainly neither of us had ever been this far west, and so the sights were new and different, and, of course, we were always comfortable around each other, having shared so much over the years.

In due course, I had us booked onto the commercial trading vessel *Carlson*, which was expected to arrive in some weeks, and was thence bound to various ports along the west African coast, making stops at Cape Town and Port Elizabeth and then on to our home Durban, of which I saw little enough due to my livelihood. Thus Hans and I had time on our hands, and then I remembered those white witch doctors of which we had heard rumors. I mentioned to Hans that I had half a mind to scout about and see if there was any substance to these rumors.

"Baas! You can go wherever you want! But I intend to stay comfortable at that rooming house you fixed up, for it reminds me of the missionary station of the Predikant, your Reverend father, where I met you years ago when you lost your way in the spirit world and arrived in this land, which is really the very last place a sane spirit would venture, but who am I to judge such things, as I am only the drunken yellow dog that the Zulu cannot be bothered with."

"Or perhaps," I said, "you've noticed that the saloon is only a couple of doors down, and one way or another you will become drunk on square-face (by square-face, he meant gin), since my moderating influence would be gone."

Hans looked struck and said, "Baas! You think so little of me, your servant!"

"It's not a matter of what I think, Hans. It is what I know."

"Well, Baas, since you put it that way, and since I promised your Reverend father, the Predikant, that I would watch over you and protect you for as long as the spirits allow—and let me tell you a secret, Baas, even after I am swept into the Place of Fires, I will bargain and cajole with whomever it is necessary to do so, so that I will still be with you, which is something you can depend on."

Thus we argued for a day or so, with Hans ever trying to change my mind about my little side expedition, and which he came close to succeeding and winning me over to his side, but then my sense returned. I said, "Be my guest if you wish to get drunk when I'm not here to get you out of your scrapes! Do as you please!"

And in the end, days later, he and I were marching south without bearers through the forested region that there served as a buffer between the town and the black jungle. My internal navigation system is usually pretty good and I seldom get lost, even in places I've never seen or ever known, but this time as forest transitioned from jungle and the sky was a great stage where various brands of air collided and rolled and changed the color of land and hills, I confess that I lost my bearings, though my plan had been simple enough, namely to keep as much as possible within sight of the majestic ocean on our right.

❀ ❀ ❀

"Baas, smell it! The sea of the west! Smell the salt!" Hans' wrinkled little face was turned upward and his nostrils quivered, and a glow spread across his face.

He was quite correct. After suffering through a maze of steamy jungle on one hand, followed by arid desert on the other, we finally found ourselves exiting a dank forest within view of a hilltop. Hans ran ahead, as he does when he is excited, and in a few moments I heard him cry out, "Baas! Come quickly."

I remember that the sound of his voice was muffled by the sea breeze that refreshed my face. I ran to the top of the hill only to find that it was not a hill at all, but a rise that fronted on and ended in a sheer cliff overlooking a small crescent-shaped bay with mighty waves crashing on the rocks far below. I then fixed my attention in the direction Hans was pointing.

"See, Baas, a great whale coming up to breathe!"

Greatly disappointed, for though I knew not what I expected, it was certainly more than a mere whale, of which I had seen many over the years. Nevertheless, I acknowledged that there certainly was a large vortex of water below.

"Hans, is that all? Have you not seen as many whales as I?"

"Yes, Baas, perhaps even more, but never have I seen such a whale as the big black brother yonder. He is a mountain, this whale, but wait, you have not seen anything but his splash. You have not seen him with your own eyes. He should rise to the surface again any moment."

Impatiently I watched the swirling waters. Then suddenly the waters parted with a mighty frothing and a titanic blue-black-maroon mottled monster fully two hundred feet in length exploded into sight, leaping straight into the air and spouting a prodigious tower of spray and foam nearly half its length across the sky.

"Great God!" I exclaimed, "Such a fish!" Just then the great whale hurled itself back into water and submerged again causing a grand swelling of the waves, and all at once its mighty double-bladed tail heaved into the air, then smoothly slipped under the churning waters.

Hans and I were mesmerized by the sight, so much so that he was speechless, which is rare enough to be sure. Even as we watched, the waves roared and parted once more and the great blunt nose of the blue-black hide poked up from the madly swirling blue-green waters, snorted a blast of spray arcing through the air, then submerged again.

Such a proud spectacle to see! Frolicking there in nature's bosom, skipping about the waters joyfully, was the earth's largest creature, the hugest fish which God ever made. The greatest of the great whales. Fully three times larger than the greatest I had ever seen. Then Hans and I found ourselves being showered with a watery mist and bits of foam as the wind carried the beast's spout up the cliff face. When it settled on the surrounding rocks, it vanished in wisps of steam. Over and again we watched that cavorting monster cross and recross that crescent bay.

But one could only be so mesmerized for so long before more practical matters intruded, and we continued on the path that would lead us to our quarry, at least as suggested by some local natives we had met.

Half a day after this, we heard faintly at the edge of our hearing, or more accurately, Hans' hearing—for his ears were more attuned than mine, and have been as long as I knew him which was long indeed, since my childhood—the distinct chug-chug of a locomotive and then a piercing whistle. Within a day we encountered the wide tracks. Hans ventured up and down the tracks for some distance but saw nothing worth reporting except more track. Insofar as it was late, I decided to throw up some prickly sage and set down our packs and rolls and make a fire, in other words to set up camp, right there near the tracks so that we would be able to learn about the train, and maybe even get a ride. Sure enough, the next morning we heard the whistle again and eventually saw a locomotive appear in the distance with one passenger car and several flat trucks loaded with equipment, all of which was covered with canvas, or oil cloth, as we could not at that distance identify its nature.

I'm sure the engineer saw our camp, but the train's momentum did not waver as it grew closer, so I said, "Hans, stand in the middle of the track and wave your arms to stop this fool train. Don't you agree that it would be at least polite for it to slow down?"

He looked at me and said, "Baas, I don't mean any disrespect for your Reverend Predikant father—who I served for years, or to you for that matter—but you can stand in front of your own damn train!"

In the end we both watched, helplessly, close alongside the track and made futile gestures. However, I don't believe that engineer would have hesitated running us down, if it came to that, for though it slowed a little in a perfect riot of squealing, sparks, steam, and the acrid stink of burnt metal, and so forth, it showed no intention of stopping, and Hans and I had to jump for our lives. As it raced past us, I noticed the name of the railroad company emblazoned on the side of the engine—Kingdom-Elias R.R.—in elaborate ornate and scrolled lettering. The mustached engineer was shaking his fist at us and had thunder in his face. As it roared by, we saw its one passenger coach along with two or three indistinct faces staring at us from within. To their credit, they seemed confused, and I gave them the benefit of the doubt.

Thereafter, assuming that the track must end somewhere, or, at the very least go through somewhere, Hans and I chose to follow the track in the direction that the train had raced off. The country all around was a patchwork of all kinds of terrain both high and low and of foliage both tropical and temperate type, but I couldn't help but be impressed that in every case, if there was a hill or other formidable obstacle in the path of the track, the train builders had drilled right through solid rock with tunnels rather than move the track around the obstacle, even in instances when the terrain included more than enough land to facilitate that approach.

For three or four days—I don't remember now, as these things do tend to blend together after a while—we continued down this deserted metal path, but a path that showed every indication of being recently created and used often enough.

Then all at once the wind shifted and Hans' little body reacted as though it was touched with a hot prod.

"Baas! I smell roasting meat—and beer! May the Predikant, your Reverend father's heaven, that he loved to talk about so long and so often, be praised for I am tired of biltong and warm water."

"Perhaps we are finally approaching the origin or destination of the railroad," I ventured. "Or perhaps that tribe of white witches is around the bend!"

But Hans had already run ahead and he didn't stop until he was out of sight due to the undulating nature of that landscape. "Hans, you monkey, come back!" I cried, but heard no response. Rather irritated at my servant for his impetuous behavior, especially as I valued his gun in this unknown territory and it was certain that two guns were better than one in the event they were needed at all. The end of it was, still following the wide track and stepping around a stand of trees, I finally found Hans, sitting on an outcrop of rock and twirling his filthy hat and grinning.

"Well, Baas, it is nice of you to finally join me, for as you can see, we have company, which can only be to the good as I am hungry and it seems that my nose did not fool me," and he gestured in the direction of the sea which was again visible from this vantage point. But that is not all I saw! Down below and in the distance a mile or so ahead and built at the bottom of a kind of valley that ended at the Atlantic Ocean, was what appeared to be a town of sorts, or village, at any rate a thriving community, or at least that was our first impression of the place as we viewed it from on high from the top of one of the cascading natural walls that formed the north face of the valley. My gaze lingered and then I spotted in the distance half hidden in the ocean mist the oddest sight.

At the far end of the community, I thought I could see through the mist a small Greek temple. But then the vision disappeared, leaving me to rub my eyes and wonder.

I said I thought there was a village or town down below us, but in a few moments I realized that the distance and the mist, or what I at first thought was mist, had deceived me. In a moment I began to understand what in fact it was that hovered below in the valley that opened to the sea! What I had interpreted as mist and dark clouds was in fact smoke billowing from heaven knows how many chimneys from numerous large buildings, which at first I took for factories. I rubbed my eyes, and looked at Hans, who was likewise studying the sight, his eyes moving rapidly, calculatingly. It is interesting how one often sees what one expects to see, rather than what actually is. Though any kind of village was unexpected, still when we saw first a cluster of buildings away in the mist, we naturally assumed on some level that the cluster was relatively contained, that is, smaller rather than larger. But when our eyes took in the sight, and expectations vanished, the vast operation below became evident. Our path fell steeply into the valley and ran straight into the middle of a veritable small city throughout which huge construction projects were underway. By far most of the activity was somewhat north-west of the city. It took me a moment to grasp the scale of the scene, but when I finally understood just what I was seeing, I counted nineteen towering steam shovels at work grabbing claw loads of rock and earth and dumping it all into a hundred or more waiting train cars that were attached to a dozen waiting steaming and smoking black locomotives, most waiting their turn. This screeching and clanging equipment was at work excavating an enormous hole in the ground, a vast bowl-shaped pit that somehow reminded me of active volcano craters or titanic meteorite craters, of which I have seen my fair share! The roar and piercing whistles of the locomotives and the cry of the earth being rent and disemboweled were horrible.

Then I saw that the clouds were made of just as much dirt and dust from the excavation as black smoke from the chimneys—and it hung over everything and severely blocked the waning late-afternoon sunlight—already turning crimson—slanting in from over the sea, casting long red shadows upon the whole scene, magnifying my impression of vulcanism. And once my brain was able to assemble all the pieces, what I saw was this: The buildings with the chimneys surrounded the pit and were arranged equidistant from one another. Massive pipes with enormous valves extended from each building and were intended, it seemed likely upon first observation, to pour some material or another into the pits, but the pipes were not active at that point.

The tracks for the trains I have mentioned were mainly laid so that they began between the "factories" and ran to the edge of the pits and were situated so that the excavators could dump their claw loads into the railcars. They mostly jutted out at first rather like the spokes of a wheel for a distance and then they all veered gently to the southeast and disappeared into the nearly opaque, poisonous, roiling red air towards wherever they dumped the debris, I suppose.

It was an uncanny sight to find this immense hub of activity where there was supposed to be nothing at all. "A tribe of white witch doctors, indeed!" I muttered to myself, which act stimulated Hans to make his first utterance since this sight had come into view.

But then, as my senses became acquainted with the waves of sensory imagery that assailed me, I blinked and stared and realized that in the distance was a second giant pit being excavated with just as much activity as the one below where Hans and I stood.

"Baas!" Hans was saying, "I am not as well-traveled as some, and Durban is as big a town as I have known, but I remember your father, the Predikant, telling stories to his poor staff about white men's kraals many times bigger than Shaka's, many times bigger than Durban, and I have never ventured out of the land of my fathers, but I do have ears and I have heard from many white men of big towns, and I suppose I am seeing such a place being born down below even now!"

"I suppose so, Hans, for such a sight is as new to me as it is to you. But be quiet now, as I need to think."

And, as it was now growing dark, Hans and I retreated and found a sheltered spot in a hollow to sleep, and at dawn we were trekking down the hill following the easiest path, as now that we saw our destination, we no longer needed to confine ourselves to following the train tracks. In so doing we traveled into some ravines and such so that we lost sight of the town for most of the distance. But toward midday, we came to the crest of a hill, and there, right before us, so close you could almost touch it, was the vital and bustling community, doing its best to live and work despite the huge disturbance and the construction going on all around it. Up close, it seemed still larger than it had from a distance. What passed for the passenger train station was off to the right, and the locomotive we had seen—it was the same because I recognized the number on its side— steaming and huffing and puffing, presumably nearly ready to move out and run down whatever poor innocent pedestrians happened to get in its way!

From our vantage point, we could look straight over the main street, which was pressed earth, with sixty or so spartan buildings with shops. At the end of the street a second street crossed and formed a T. At that crossroads and facing down the main street was the tallest building that was within our view. Perhaps two hundred men and women were on the streets, none strolling, each with a mission and walking with purpose in various directions. None seemed to be taking in the sights. There was no loitering in this place. Despite the crowd, the ebb and flow of its movements were remarkably organized, and I felt that the architects of this mysterious metropolis knew what they were doing and had planned well.

In addition, I was amazed to see that a dwarf-sized railroad system crisscrossed the town—a miniature railroad system with tiny engines and cars. This turned out to be a transportation system, a handy way to move people and equipment around within the limits of the town. The locomotives were perhaps ten feet in length, yet looking for all the world like their big brothers that hauled rubble from the pits. These were driven by men and women who rode the engines much as they would ride horses, their legs hugging and pressing hard into either side of the black metal engines. All in all, it proved to be a very efficient tram system.

In a moment, Hans was pulling at my sleeve, and he said reflectively, "Baas, do you see someplace where they sell square-face, for I am thirsty, and what is the use of a town like this unless it has a saloon?"

I inspected what I could see and had to admit that there didn't appear to be a saloon, at least within our view. But I ventured a guess. "Maybe that tall building has something of the sort."

Well there was nothing for it but to continue ahead, but before we started, I peered into the distance, hoping to see the temple that I'd noticed the day before, but I couldn't see anything of the sort. In a couple of hours, we emerged from the undergrowth through which we had traversed onto a road paved with stone. This led into the town, which was just ahead. But now I noticed a queer fact that was not obvious from the distance. The entire town had a tall fence around it, and as we got closer, I saw that there was a fence within a fence and that it all bristled with barbs, such as you hear about being used on American cattle ranches. And every few yards there were guard towers and armed guards, as though the place was a prison camp. Yet, from what we could see from the distance, the populace, while seemingly industrious, also seemed free to go their own ways.

Frankly I was more than a little confused.

In a few minutes, around a curve and at end of the road, we saw a guard's station and gate with three stout fellows in military uniforms, but of a stripe I was not familiar with.

"Baas, what do you suppose these big men are guarding? And do you see their many brothers with guns on those towers? Perhaps it is gold or diamonds, but then again not even the Bank of Durban has so many guards. What could be more valuable then gold or diamonds?"

"Our skins for one thing," I suggested.

"O, Baas, that's easy for you to say, for you are the great Macumazana, but I am only a shriveled yellow monkey as the Great One never fails to remind both of us, and the skin of a monkey is hardly worth more than a rusty nail!"

"Hans, you are worth more than a rusty nail to me, even if you are shriveled."

"Baas, yes, you are right. I am worth more to you because I have saved your life more times than I can remember."

"Perhaps that is so, Hans, but I have saved your skin just as many times!"

By then we had marched right up to the guard shack.

The tallest of the three guards questioned us, or I should say questioned me, in the manner that all such men question the arrival of unexpected newcomers. I explained that I was Allan Quatermain and that Hans was with me, and that we had come out of the jungle after a very long trek from

"Hans, you are worth more than a rusty nail to me, even if you are shriveled."

Central Africa and that we were there only because we had stumbled on the place by accident and insofar as it was the first sign of civilization that we'd encountered, would it be too much to ask to be treated with civility and be offered food and drink at the least?

The spokesman looked doubtful, but at least he was not belligerent, and sent one of his colleagues off with a message. I suppose he would have been within his rights to have sent us packing, so I counted our blessings—at least in the beginning!

Hans and I waited in the hot sun. Hans sat on the ground in what shade he could find, but I was too proud and stood on principle. Literally. We waited thus for almost an hour. I could see that our presence there had aroused the curiosity of passersby on the other side of the double fence, but nobody did more than slacken their walking pace a bit, stare a moment, then continue about their business. My patience was running thin, when finally I spotted two men approach the gate from the inside. The gates were opened for them, and they came through and advanced up to me.

The man who seemed to be the leader was about my size, that is to say, rather small, but he had a high forehead with a slightly receding hairline, long swept-back grey hair and long extremely bushy grey mutton-chop whiskers, which were quite the rage back then. His hair and beard were so profuse that they connected with hardly a trace of facial skin showing except a little on either side of his nose and around his eyes. The other man was about the same age but had a rounder face, that is, they both seemed about 40 years of age, though the second man sported a trim beard, rather like mine, in fact. This first man came right up to me and held out his hand, which for the sake of politeness I took and shook in the accepted European manner. I make this specification because when one lives in Africa as long as I have, one learns that the common handshake is not by any means a common method of greeting, and, in fact, how one presents one's hands at the beginning of an acquaintance could well spell the difference between life and death. Also, I had reservations about simply greeting the man, particularly after his having made us wait in the sun for an hour. He spoke and I was surprised by his strong Scottish accent:

"Allan Quatermain! I have heard of you. Yes, I dare say, that there are few who reside on this continent who have not heard of the great white hunter!"

I often hear this sort of remark, or compliment as I suppose it is intended to be, but learned long ago not to take it seriously, for if I did, my head would swell and I could not fit into any of my hats again! But more than that, such things that are heard about me are usually second or third hand and generally not representative of the real me. Thus I chose to ignore his remarks and said, "Sir, I am afraid that you have me at a disadvantage."

Naturally this always embarrasses the speaker, which put me back on top of the social order, and indeed, this is exactly what happened. Blushing, he said, "Forgive me, Quatermain, but my name is James Maxwell, James Clerk Maxwell." He stopped and showed every sign that his name ought to have been familiar to me and that I ought to have been impressed. But since neither was the case, I merely looked back at him with a blank face. Then he quickly motioned toward his companion and said, "And this is Giovanni Schiaparelli," and seemed again to wait for some sort of reaction.

Of course, this second name meant as little to me as the first. Schiaparelli didn't speak, so I could only guess that he was Italian. I nodded to him and said to Maxwell, "Mr. Maxwell, obviously I can't help but wonder what all this is about. None of this is supposed to be here, or certainly I would know of it."

"Yes, yes. We are involved in some research of a scientific nature, and we established this laboratory only a few months ago. Just a moment, please." Here, he and Schiaparelli moved off and whispered together for several minutes. Then Schiaparelli went back in the direction they had come, hurrying through the gate without saying a word to us, and Maxwell returned. "You know, Quatermain, we don't normally have callers, as you can imagine, and I wish I could be more gracious, but I must cut this interview short. I'm terribly glad we had an opportunity to meet, however briefly. Where are you off to now?"

Taken aback by both his attitude and the question, I think I sputtered some sort of response that I cannot recall. Hans took me by the elbow and said in Dutch, "Baas, I don't understand why these men are being rude and did not invite us inside so that we could rest our feet, have some cool drink, and even offer us a place to lay our poor heads." I couldn't have agreed with him more, and was about to say so, when his bloodshot eyes grew round and his wrinkled old face beamed and he smiled, whereupon he said, "Say, Baas! That merciful Spirit of which your Reverend father, the Predikant, never ceased to remind all us poor servants who manned his station, has looked down from his throne, or up from the Place of Fires, I know not which, and has seen our sad case and has come to our rescue!"

"Hans," I responded, "stop your nonsense and let us make ready to leave this inhospitable place."

But the little Hottentot continued his gaping, and said, "It may be nonsense, Baas, but I think you will think otherwise when I tell you that I see someone who will make this sick looking white man swallow his thick tongue. See over there, through that crowd there, there is a face we know well, very well, indeed, leaving that building."

Shaking my head in befuddlement, I followed Hans' pointed finger, and, indeed, spotted not only a familiar face but a dear one as well.

"Maxwell," I said to the man, "before my servant and I turn around to go, having been turned away by a degree of insensitivity rare, indeed, nearly unprecedented, in a civilized man, please note that I see an old friend inside your fence whose attention I would like to catch, if you don't mind."

He looked off in the direction I had indicated and seemed puzzled. "Excuse me?" Maxwell said.

And seeing that she was about to round the corner of a building, I called out loudly, "Maria! Maria Mitchell! Professor Mitchell!" which succeeded in getting her attention. She looked our way, double-took, stared, smiled, no, grinned broadly, waved, and rushed over to the gate.

"Allan Quatermain! My God! It is so good to see you! How did you know to look for me here? It is so good to see you! And Hans! Neither of you look one iota different since our Abyssinian adventure last year. Well, perhaps it is closer to two years." Then to Maxwell, "Well, Doctor, what is going on here? Don't you know Allan Quatermain?" There followed an awkward exchange between the two, with Maria finally putting her foot down and demanding, "What are you waiting for? I insist that you escort these men through immediately!"

The previous year, I had been hired by several British gentlemen to take them to Ethiopia, which at that time I had never visited. It was while on that earlier expedition that our path crossed with Professor Mitchell and her party, and it worked out that the two expeditions were merged before we plunged south into that desert for reasons it's not necessary to go into now. The point being that Maria is an American astronomer, and we were well-acquainted, and it was the purest serendipity that Hans had spotted her just at that particular moment.

Well, there was a bit of give and take, with the guards pointing out some particulars of their bylaws and about the minutia of our arrival, and

Maxwell holding quite firm.

It was pretty much of a stalemate, when another man approached the gate from the inside and, muttering something to the guards on that side, passed through just as Maria attached herself to him, so that, in a flash they both had come outside and she began exchanging affectionate greetings with me, and also Hans.

This new fellow was yet another with a beard, not as full as Maxwell's nor as well-trimmed as Schiaparelli's. However, he seemed utterly out of place as he was attired formally in tall shiny top hat and tails and smoked a cigar.

"Hello, Maria, won't you introduce me to your friend?"

"Where have you been Impey?" replied Maria, not responding to the inquiry. "I have been looking for you for days."

"Didn't anyone tell you, I was tying up some loose ends 'over yonder.'" This was the first reference that I heard to the mysterious "over yonder," which while not mentioned often, would occasionally slip out in hushed tones, succeeding in rousing the curiosity of both Hans and me at the outset of this adventure.

"Well never mind. You're here now. Impey, this is my old friend Allan Quatermain. You cannot imagine the scrapes we've been through together!" Here she winked at me, and in my mind's eye I saw her swinging and jabbing a glass sword—decapitating a Danikil tribesman two years before!

"And Allan, this is Impey Barbicane! He sent a missile to the moon five or six years ago. You may have read about it. He is the world's greatest engineer—the chief engineer and architect of all this." Her hand gestured in all directions.

"Maria, that's not entirely true. Isambard Kingdom Brunel's work inspired much of what I have done!"

Now there was a name I had heard of and was impressed with, even having been isolated at the bottom of Africa from the stream of technology that Britain seemed consumed with. Brunel had built some of the greatest ships of his day, the Great Western and Great Eastern among them, and the Great Western Railroad, not to mention gigantic tunnels that crossed under rivers, and enormous bridges that crossed over them. Now that I had heard Brunel's name, a little of the mystery I was feeling faded, as Brunel was quite adept at building the impossible. Though Brunel had died some years before, it was clear to me then that this man Barbicane must have been a protégé.

Anyway, the end result of this exchange was that Maria won the day and Hans and I were shepherded in.

Before long we were established in the tall building that we had seen from a distance, which, while not a hotel in the normal sense of the word, nevertheless served a similar function and we called it that out of convenience, and Hans and I had the grand opportunity to bathe and refresh—or rather, I did, for water seldom touched my manservant except when it was necessary to ford some wild stream or another. This building was typical of the rest of the structures in this so-called laboratory, as Maxwell had called it, that is, the building was made of freshly sawn lumber and other rude materials and had clearly been thrown together in great haste. Indeed, the whole laboratory was being constructed in front of our eyes!

When we, that is, Maria and I, met again, it was in what passed for a sitting room of the hotel. Hans was there of course, but he preferred to plant himself unobtrusively in the corner as he was wont to do. Maria and I did not just then have the opportunity to converse in private as Maxwell soon joined us, and then it was time for tea.

During that ever-so-civilized ceremony, Maria suggested to Maxwell, "James, Allan's discretion is second to none. In fact, there are things that we have experienced together (here she looked meaningfully at me) that even you have never dreamt of, and of which neither he nor I can ever speak, as we have given our oaths."

"That may well be, Professor Mitchell, but we have a responsibility to discharge, and until such time that is accomplished, there is no room for any who were not invited and who have no professional credentials to speak of. And besides, we ourselves have all given our own oaths with regard to our project."

"Well, then," she said, "I suppose my services and my specific areas of expertise are not needed." She stood, and said to me, "Come, Allan, please wait for me to pack some essentials and I will join you." Maxwell also stood, a courteous reflex I suppose. Maria walked up to him and stood eyeball to eyeball!

"Professor, that is not acceptable!" Maxwell said. "If for no other reason, I cannot allow a woman to trek through that horrid wilderness outside our gates!"

At that, Maria laughed heartily! "Ha! James, I assure you that that 'wilderness,' as you call it, is nothing at all compared to the places that Allan and I have shared! That jungle beyond our fences and those desert sands are as formidable as this tea-party, I assure you!" As she spoke, she stared into the man's face.

Taken aback, Dr. Maxwell could only gulp air for a few moments as he composed himself. "Maria, notwithstanding the dangers outside, this project needs your experience and abilities for good reason, and it would be a great disadvantage to our group if you were to leave us."

"Wonderful, then I want your promise that, in due course, Allan will be allowed to know what we are doing." Then she looked at me, embarrassed.

"Allan, I'm sorry, but I assume too much! I was so happy to see you that it didn't occur to me that you only happened upon this place by chance and that you have your own plans. I don't mean to impose on you or force information upon you that you would rather not know."

"Professor Mitchell," I said, "no plans I have are so important that I can't delay them to spend time with a charming dear friend." Here she blushed and I regretted my impertinence.

"Very good, it is settled!" Maria had said. "James, until which time as Allan can be told the essentials, please let my friends" (here she turned and looked at Hans pointedly for Maxwell's sake) "have the freedom to move as they please through the laboratory."

"Why do you call this place a laboratory?" I asked.

Maxwell responded: "Well, rightfully, that is what it is. It certainly doesn't have any claim to permanence, though. This is all a temporary arrangement built to support our special studies. It is indeed a scientific laboratory."

"I cannot wait until I know something more about your purpose here, Doctor Maxwell. Professor Mitchell called you thus. I should hope I'll avoid getting ill during my stay, as I would not wish to impose on you."

"Oh, no, Allan," Maria exclaimed. "Doctor Maxwell is the world's greatest living physicist."

Now it was Maxwell's turn to blush. "I wouldn't go that far, Professor Mitchell. Certainly I learned from the great Faraday himself."

"Don't be modest, James." She turned to me and said, "James is the world's authority on electricity and magnetism, and has shown that they are interrelated in what he has called the electromagnetic field. James' brand new tome, *A Treatise on Electricity and Magnetism*, was published only this year, and there are those that say that it will transform the world!"

"Maria, please!" groaned Maxwell.

"Furthermore, James is this laboratory's chief scientist and all aspects of the work here not related specifically to building and engineering are his responsibility."

And that was only the beginning or our adventure. I am generally impervious to matters that stun other men. That's because I have seen and experienced so much during my time in South Africa. Nevertheless, I was thunderstruck at being in the presence such an assortment. What on earth could two renowned astronomers (for I am worldly enough to know that that is Giovanni Schiaperelli's field) and the world's greatest physicist plus the world's greatest living engineer, all be doing in an isolated and well-guarded facility on the west coast of Africa?

Well, there is so much more to tell. In the coming days, I met many famous and notable scientists. (Or so I would determine them to be in later years as I happened across their names in newspapers, or in other sundry manners. Among them were some astonishingly bright young men who had been drafted right out of school to aid in this endeavor—youngsters named Edison, Hertz, John Thomson, Nikola Tesla, Max Planck, and others.) The core of the team consisted of a number of absolutely dedicated astronomers, physicists, and engineers, all specialists in the narrow fields of electricity, magnetism, and electromagnetic waves. It was quite a select group. It seemed all the world's most brilliant men in these fields had been brought to this one small area. Of course, one can't help but wonder why this was so. What on earth could possibly have prompted all these geniuses to have come together in this manner? Well it took some time for me to glean any part of it, with Maria's help; still I am not at all sure that I really had any idea of what went on there during all the time Hans and I were detained—yes, detained, for in the end, once we were let in, we were not allowed to leave, much to Maria's chagrin.

Hans and I had been there only a few days when the first thing of consequence, from our perspective, occurred. During this time we were never told anything, nor could I even imagine what was going on all around me. The excavation of the pits and the construction of the laboratory went on ceaselessly. The constant smoke and dust made breathing difficult. There was a sort of class structure in place. The scientists and their assistants lived and worked in the main laboratory grounds that we knew from first hand knowledge, but the laborers and skilled craftsmen lived in separate areas and were transported by trains.

As I've already said, there were trains everywhere. And these were of three types. There were the ordinary trains with carriages of the type that you see coming into and leaving a busy urban train depot, though these were neither ornate nor plush and largely utilitarian—spartan I think is the word. The one that almost ran us down was of this sort. Then, of course, there were the dozens of work engines that hauled away the debris deposited by the huge excavators busy at the two pits.

And then there were also the miniature trains that I mentioned before. These were utterly unique, and, frankly, captivated both Hans and me. The entire laboratory, or at least the part we would inhabit for the duration, was crisscrossed with a web of tiny tracks on which traveled this miniaturized railroad system, which, as I had seen earlier, carried people from place to place. Instead of horse-drawn hansoms and carriages and omnibuses, this place had small electric trains pulled by tiny smokeless locomotives on which there was installed a kind of saddle to seat the drivers, both men and women, who had available an array of levers and knobs and wheels—and best of all, bells and whistles that they used to warn pedestrians and which neither Hans nor I ever ceased to enjoy hearing. Behind the engines, there were attached a dozen or so small open cars, each holding fifteen or twenty people on benches. And of course these trains had regular stops, though one could always wave one down or ask the driver—engineer?—to make unscheduled stops.

By the way, eventually I learned, and was astonished to find out, that the population of the laboratory and its work crew and their families, all of which required this complicated transit system numbered somewhere in the neighborhood of 40,000! Most of whom we never saw, as they were busy out of sight.

During breakfast of our fourth or fifth day there, with Maria, Maxwell, Barbicane, and myself at a table overlooking the Atlantic Ocean. I ventured, "Professors, Mr. Barbicane, as we approached this—laboratory—from atop the hill, we thought we saw something odd off in the distance to the south. It seemed to be a columned structure, a sort of temple, or at least that is how it registered in my humble mind, through the mist or smoke."

Maria and Barbicane looked at one another and smiled, then Maria said, "Allan, what you saw is an interesting aspect of this place. Come, Impey and I will show you." They looked at Maxwell, but he said he was needed at the workshop.

In a few minutes, Barbicane, Hans, Maria, and I were waiting outside for a westbound miniature train. We boarded and rode it through the main part of the laboratory.

When our conveyance reached the outskirts of the place and began

...this place had small electric trains pulled by tiny smokeless locomotives...

its return leg, Barbicane asked the engineer to stop, whereupon we got off and strode through a guarded gate much as the one by which we had entered several days earlier and I was reminded how heavily guarded the facility was! We found a gravel path that we continued on for a half mile or so ducking in and out of stands of trees. Very soon we heard a roaring very like a waterfall, and smelt a tang in the air. The path entered a glade, and there in the middle of the glade stood the totally anomalous sight of a temple, for want of a better word. It was circular and comprised of ten columns. It stood thirty-five or forty feet high with an inside column-to-column diameter of about twenty feet. It looked Roman or Greek, I'm sorry but I've never been educated to tell the difference. It stood in the middle of a broad circular pool with half a dozen shooting fountains.

The path we were on led to a footbridge and we crossed over the pool to the temple itself. There squarely in the middle between the pillars was a sort of circular well comprised of a wall about four feet high, and when we looked over the wall into the well, we saw and heard and smelled huge volumes of water spouting from two pipes in the well's sides. The sound was thunderous! I'm sure that millions of gallons a day must have crashed out of those pipes mingling and plunging down the 20-foot-deep, blue-tiled well. I cast my eyes downward, savoring the power of the raging waters. I stood entranced and wrapped in spray, delighting in the wonder of it all.

"Maria," I finally asked, "what is this place? What is the meaning of all this?" By which I meant the whole massive enterprise, of course; but I was not yet to receive a direct answer. Instead Maria looked at Barbicane who said: "Quatermain, you have not seen anything yet, as you have been here only a few days, but you will soon see and learn things on a scale never before conceived by the mind of man. What we are doing here makes my experiment of sending a manned projectile to the moon and back again look like a mere backyard romp. Let me say for now that we who are involved in this project are performing an experiment that requires an enormous amount of energy. Vast amounts! As a consequence, we…well…invented a system that creates electricity in quantities inconceivable before now except perhaps by the mind of God. Where, you ask, does such electricity come from? Well it so happens that electricity can most conveniently be produced by the downhill rush of millions of gallons of water. Thus our engineers, to the purpose of diverting and harnessing immense quantities of water, built a titanic dam high up in the Loma mountains two hundred miles to the east, damming the Rokel River and turning a convenient valley into a reservoir. They are the Columbiad Dam and the Columbiad Reservoir, respectively (named after the cannon that was central to my Luna project). To control the flow of the water released from the reservoir a huge gravity-driven network of eleven further dams and reservoirs, tunnels, pump stations, aqueducts and water conveyance pipelines were also built, all of which move three hundred million gallons per day and generate over two billion kilowatt hours per year of hydropower electricity, which is transmitted here via a two hundred mile long network of power stations housing generators, transformers, and dynamos—machines that never previously existed—not to mention the power lines that funnel it all here.

"So, to answer your question," Barbicane continued brightly, "we built this temple—we call it the Atlantis Water Temple—as a monument to that effort. Right here, this very spot, is the terminus of the underground water pipe that begins near Mount Bintumani. This is the final destination of the Rokel River water, water that is spawned by the dense rainforests water skirting the Loma Mountains. When it flows out of this well, you can see that it is expelled into the ocean, for it is not the water that is needed, but the electric power it generates. It was all completed just a few months ago, even though, amazingly, it was only conceived and designed two years ago!"

"Two years!" I cried. "Surely something so vast would require decades of effort and more money than I can begin to conceive of."

"Yes, Allan, that is so—unless there is a well-to-do patron, sufficient motivation, and a clear deadline," Maria said.

What can one say when confronted with such staggering information? Standing there I literally shook from the shock. My companions seemed to understand and gave me a moment to pull myself together. Then I spotted a legend that had been carved into the stone above the columns. It was Latin and read:

IN ASTRIS ES VESTRI POTENTIA ET GLORIA

I asked Maria what that meant and she told me: "In the stars are found your power and glory."

After a pause, I said, "A moment ago, I asked what all this is about? Mr. Barbicane has answered in a manner I could never have imagined in a hundred years, but what I meant to ask was: What is this place? I mean the whole laboratory? Why are you here?"

She looked at Barbicane who could only shrug. Then she said, "Allan, notwithstanding my having taken your side recently, let me say that the details are not for me to share. For now, I can say that we are performing some electrical experiments that include an aspect of astronomy, which of course, explains my presence. Come, let's take a walk so I can hear myself think." She needed to raise her voice over the din of the roaring water. Just then Barbicane made his excuses and went off, leaving me alone with Maria. We then continued on the trail on the farther side of the temple.

Of course, Hans was there, too, but unobtrusively as was his tendency when discussion ascended into realms beyond his comprehension (and frankly beyond mine, as well, if truth be known, but I had the knack of being able to look interested or at least to keep a poker face)—but I was saying that Hans kept to himself.

When we had walked to a spot on the trail that was quieter—and drier, too, as the air around the well was forever filled with a cool mist—Maria began to fill me in: "I was asked to join this project not long after my return to Vassar College from Ethiopia, and when I arrived here, construction of the buildings had only just begun. I've been here at the laboratory now for only about eight months, but when I arrived here, there were only a few shacks and a beach."

Frankly, what she had just said was far more than I could comprehend, but then an image flashed into my head that helped me grasp the vastness of what she was saying.

"I suppose," I said, "it wouldn't be far different from Field-Marshal Lord Napier's Ethiopian campaign—the history of which you recall was an important factor in our last experiences together: 280 ships, 32,000 men, 20,000 mules, and vast amounts of materiel and they set up shop on a beach and—boom!—a small city sprang into being overnight. Locomotives were hauled in, and elephants, and huge piers were built. Remembering that, it doesn't surprise me at all that so much has happened here so fast!"

"Excellent, Allan. Frankly I had not thought of that, but it is an excellent analogy."

Now that I had a picture in my head that worked for me, I continued, "I have so many questions. What are the pits that are being dug? Is it more construction, or are they looking for something? What is it all for? Something to do with astronomy, but how could anything require as much energy as you tell me is being generated. And the aqueduct you described would take years and millions to plan and build. It is all impossible, yet here it is before my eyes!"

Maria looked very serious and then said, "Well, what I can tell you is that we are building a telescope, a very special telescope, one like the world has never seen."

"A telescope!" I cried. "All this for a telescope!" Of course, the telescope I saw in my mind's eye was a tube such as one held up to one's eye.

"Actually, Allan, we are involved in a project as big as the world, quite literally. The instrument that is being built here has no comparison. And that instrument, that is, the telescope, is at the heart of this project."

"That is all well and good, but why are you here, Maria?

"Well Allan, after our adventure in Abyssinia, I returned to Vassar, where, as you know, my role has been to teach something of the stars and planets to inquisitive young women. However, because of the meteorite specimens I brought back, I became a bit of a celebrity and received many invitations to present at schools in Boston, Pennsylvania, New York, and the like. Also I wrote and submitted, and had published, half a dozen papers to scientific journals, and I was quite pleased with the response from the science community. Of course there were a few naysayers who accused me of everything from carelessness to outright fraud. However, I'm happy to report that on balance, my supporters were legion. I had been back about six months, and then one day I received by courier an unexpected proposal. That letter alerted me that I would soon be invited to join a special project. There was no description of either the project or my proposed responsibilities. Though I ignored the note, a few weeks afterward another courier appeared at my door, and this time the message offered some particulars about comets that grabbed my attention. It seemed that these were of particular interest to the people who wished me to join them. Of course, they could not have chosen a better ploy: I became fascinated, but still hesitant, as my responsibility lay just where I was, especially as I had only recently been away for a prolonged time.

"Here is where they offered an inducement that could not be ignored. They offered to build a new observatory on the Vassar Campus on the condition that the experiment they were conducting achieved the desired result. Well, what was I to do? I believed that these people made the proposal in good faith, as the college board was already meeting with their representatives by the time I made up my mind to pursue the invitation. In time I had boarded the steamship *de Grandin*. My destination was the Greenwich Observatory. When I arrived, I received the surprise of my life. At the observatory I was received by James Clerk Maxwell himself! He told me that he had selected me especially and that I had been brought over for the sole purpose of his asking me personally if I wanted to join a select group of physicists and astronomers who were gathering in West Africa to conduct a vital experiment. Allan! James is probably the most esteemed living scientist. Whatever residual concerns I still had about this enterprise, regardless of what it truly was, evaporated on the spot, and I became a dedicated member of the team. Very quickly after my arrival here, machine shops were built with the ability to produce the most sophisticated, delicate instrumentalities imaginable with complex components, even devices for computational work based on the engines of Charles Babbage." She was quiet for a time and merely gestured all around. "I am anxious to see what will become of it all."

By this time, our little walk around the temple had concluded and we passed through the guard gates and returned to the laboratory. Once inside, Hans, who had accompanied us on this whole astonishing tour, but who had not said a word, and thus I had almost forgotten he was with us, spoke quietly in Zulu to me, "Baas, I have seen and heard this day much more than I could ever care to. And, as you know, I understand nothing this fine lady ever says. Whenever we are around her, my head feels stuffed with babble and pains me, and it seems to me that she is about to tell you still more that will undoubtedly be far more than your poor old Hottentot servant would ever want to hear. Thus I will occupy myself looking for what passes for square-face in this poor place!" At which point he scurried around the corner of a building before I could put in a word one way or another.

Maria noticed Hans' exit and looked at me questioningly, but I only shrugged. Then a messenger ran up to her with a note in an envelope. She read it, seemed delighted and said, "Allan, you are being invited to the workshop. Maybe they will now explain rather more to you."

Maria took me to a low building that didn't seem to have a door or windows at ground level, or none that I could see, and we descended some stairs to reach an entrance. Once inside, there were more stairs going down and then we were far below ground. We went down a hallway and through some double doors, and thus entered a room—a room they called the workshop—wherein Maxwell was in the midst of writing some mathematic calculations on a large board and lecturing to the many men in attendance, including Barbicane, but stopped when he noticed we had entered.

Maria didn't waste her time nor her breath. "James, I hope you intend to give Allan some information so he doesn't stew in his curiosity. Allan needs to understand what we are doing here. I just explained how I was lured here against my will." She smiled as she said this.

"I see," he said, looking rather unhappy and looking at Barbicane, who nodded. "Well, Mr. Quatermain, since you are here and a close friend of Maria's, we'll let you in on what we are doing. I can give you an overview now. It is an exercise in astronomy that is quite well-funded by an agency that would prefer to keep its identity secret for now.

Then, Maxwell paused and reflected and seemed confused. "Well, Quatermain, I hardly know where to begin or how to explain it all."

"Where to begin—?" Maxwell repeated, mumbling. He looked at Maria. "Have you mentioned anything of the mechanical nature of our work?"

"Well," Maria said, "I said that we were building a kind of telescope ..."

To which Maxwell said to me, "Well, but of course that probably wouldn't mean much to you, I suppose...so I suppose the easiest thing to do is to explain the whole thing chronologically." Here he stepped over to one of the many bookshelves in the room, and took down a Bible. (Incidentally, the people who know me also know that I pride myself in my knowledge of the Old Testament.) Anyway, he opened the book to where there was a ribbon bookmark and opened his mouth as if to begin to read, but instead he looked at me first and said, "Matthew, chapter two."

Then he read, "'Now when Jesus was born in Bethlehem of Judea in the days of Herod the king, behold, wise men from the East came to Jerusalem, saying, "Where is he who has been born king of the Jews? For we have seen his star in the East, and we have come to worship him.'" His finger ran down a few lines and he continued, "'. . . lo, the star which they had seen in the East went before them, till it stood over where the child was. When they saw the star, they rejoiced exceedingly with great joy; and going into the house they saw the child with Mary his mother, and they fell down and worshipped him.'"

He slapped the book shut and looked at me. I shrugged and said, "Yes, the Nativity...and...?"

"The point of interest here is the star—the Star of Bethlehem. It is astonishing how many myriads of men have devoted unfathomable amounts of energy into trying to understand the nature of that star." Here Maxwell sighed deeply. "So very much time and energy and effort has been dedicated in attempts to understand those few words that are mentioned almost in passing in the gospel. Of course there are those who claim that the author of Matthew (you know, of course, that the apostle Matthew probably was dead and gone when this gospel was composed late in the first century and, therefore, the gospel can be thought of as a kind of forgery...) simply made it all up and there was never any star or magi or any of the rest." He paused and shrugged before he went on.

"I don't pretend to know one way or another; nevertheless, we have been charged to conduct this experiment under the assumption that it is true. In a nut shell, all this is intended to study the Star of Bethlehem, and we are building a special kind of telescope in order to do just that." Here he paused.

Frankly, I did not know how to respond. I certainly was never one of those men who expended much on that point. I had never given the Star of Bethlehem any thought at all. It simply was part of the festivities that made up Christmas, along with trees and ornaments, ribbons, toys and children. The star was always shiny with rays of light, usually depicted by a circle of pointed beams. I certainly had never considered that it might be something that anybody would want to study. But instead of saying any of that, I said, "And...?"

※ ※ ※

Just as Maxwell was concluding his ridiculous business about the Star of Bethlehem, I noticed that Hans had made an appearance. He was standing by the door to the workshop, trying not to be noticed in his typical chameleon manner of blending into his surroundings—yet at the same time gesturing frantically to me. When I felt I could politely withdraw to the side of the room where he was, I excused myself to find out what sort of trouble my servant had got himself into. I found him to be sopping wet!

"Hans, how on earth did you find me, and what happened to you?"

"Never mind that, Baas! You know I have my ways! Baas! Listen. This will not be the ordinary sort of chatter, chatter by reason of which the Great One takes great pleasure calling your servant a little yellow monkey, or dog, depending on his mood. Again, listen! Not finding any square-face in this place which is so like so many army barracks, and I admit I didn't look that hard because I knew that if I was lucky enough to find some, I would doubtlessly do something foolish and then you would find cause to be angry with me, and of course I didn't want that to happen—"

"Not that that ever stopped you before!" I interrupted.

But he seemed not to notice and rambled on: "I decided to visit that place that our teacher lady friend and that tall fellow with the tall hat who spoke funny [referring to Barbicane's American accent I supposed] took us, the place of the crashing waters. I was looking into the waters and then thought I saw something sparkling down at the bottom. I looked and I looked again and again and I felt certain that there was really something shiny down there—not like the visions I sometimes swear to have seen when I've had too much square-face, which as you know all too well is truly seldom."

"Get to the point, man, or I will find reason to get angry with you right here and now," I said grinning all the while, but also being conscious that my absence from the group was causing some looks to be cast our way.

"Well, Baas, my curiosity got the best of me and I decided to take a look, but I knew that if I jumped into that whirlpool that I would be instantly swept out into that hole high in the cliff that dumps into the sea, at least we were told of such a hole and I doubt not its existence or the fact that if I were to be swept out of it, I would be dropped far into the ocean and you would never find me again, or if you did I would most certainly be broken and crushed and have joined your Reverend father, the Predikant, in the Place of Fires. So I hurried back through the guard gate as they knew me and I found a stout rope and returned to the spot, made the rope fast to the thick tree branch you saw me pick up this morning and which I used as a staff such as I've seen pictures of Moses do in the Book that your Reverend father, the Predikant, showed often to all those on the station when they had the time. Then I placed the pole across the top of the well, secured myself as I know that Baas would want me to and climbed down where the current nearly swept me away, but luckily I had wrapped both ankles and wrist securely to the rope and was able to get my balance. Then I held my nose and went deep into the water head first and felt around with my hands in search of whatever the shining object should be. Well, after a time and trying several times, in the end, and seeming like I had half-drowned, I caught hold of it and climbed back to safety. When I saw what I had caught, I forgot the rope and all else and raced back here to find you."

"Well, what is it? What was worth all that trouble?"

"Just this, Baas." Then his hand dropped into his pocket and he pulled out an object palm up. My surprise was total, and what can I say but this was like life—my life, the tree of my whole life—had just been topped by a shining star! A star unimaginable! Hans was holding out to me a huge natural diamond—far, far larger than a hen's egg! Immediately I recognized it as probably the largest diamond ever found. I quickly grabbed it from Hans' grubby hands and slipped it into my own pocket. I was speechless. Perhaps I even cried. I could hear my heart pounding in my chest. Hans looked frightened.

"Baas! What are we to do? I didn't think that anything so shiny could turn my belly so! I think, that now that you have seen it, it would be best to throw it back where I found it."

"Are you out of your mind?" I asked harshly through my teeth, trying to be inconspicuous.

"Baas, is there something wrong with your mouth suddenly? It is all twisted?"

"Well, what do you expect? Suddenly we are millionaires and set for life. It's the most outrageous and wonderful thing that could ever have happened."

"Well, perhaps you are a millionaire. But for myself I would rather be the trusted servant of a good shot, and if I had to, then I would prefer to be the servant of a good shot who happens to be a millionaire. I still say we ought to throw it back where we—that is I—found it."

"Stop being so foolish!"

Luckily, by this time the sun was getting low, and, since Maxwell's lecture seemed to have reached a conclusion, I could naturally plead exhaustion. It was dark and we went off, with Hans trailing behind, to the hotel where we had long settled in.

❋ ❋ ❋

The next morning, we were both up early, which is normal for us. Hans insisted on taking me to the temple to show me exactly how he had found the stone. However, just as we were passing through the gate, Maria caught up to us, to my dismay, as I wanted just then to hear Hans' story alone. However, she and I fell into conversation. As we approached the temple, which commands a view of sea, Hans ran ahead to the cliff's edge, as he forever does when there is the possibility of something exciting ahead, just like a child.

"Baas! Baas! Lady Baas! Over here, You must see this with your own eyes." Suddenly he was shouting, and the whole scene gave me a weird sense of déjà vu!

We rushed around the temple and through the forest where there was a path and joined my servant. "Baas! Look, do your eyes see what mine see?" And he was pointing and gesticulating wildly. When I looked in the direction he was indicating, frankly, I couldn't believe my eyes.

"Baas! The whale we saw the other day, there it is again, or its twin brother. And its game has changed. It has risen and is asleep on the water's surface."

Sure enough, I looked down and saw that the sea waters were calm and devoid of ocean surf, and there it was, that marvelous gargantuan whale we had spied at the outset. It was down below and it did seem to have come to rest.

"Surely it is exhausted," said Hans. "In fact, I too, in its place, would need to rest after such sport as we saw, Baas! Can you imagine its weight? But look: it seems to have died. Yes, already it is stiff. As still as a ship at anchor. Death must have come quickly. Our monstrous friend must have been a fool for a whale or a very old man!"

Dumbfounded, I could only lamely mutter, "Yes, but in either case it clearly over-exerted itself."

I turned to Maria, who was by my side. As her reaction was only to wear an inexplicable smile, I turned back to the scene with the whale.

"Oh, you have spotted one of our little toys! Gentlemen, meet the *Nova*, the king of the seas!"

I looked at her hopelessly, my jaw dropped open. "What? Toy? Toy? What do you mean?" And then I suddenly realized what the truth must be. "You mean that's a ship? A ship that you built?"

"Well I didn't build it personally, of course, but Impey supervised its construction based on some documents that were—well, uncovered." Here she seemed to struggle to hide a smile.

"Is that what all this is about?"

Here Maria almost looked at me pityingly. "Do you forget so fast that we are bound to study Christ's star. The *Nova* is merely a tool to help us build our telescope."

Frankly I could not speak, and for once in his life, neither could Hans!

"Come, Allan, your seeing the *Nova* was probably premature, and I think that Maxwell will need to explain this part of the puzzle as well!"

"Perhaps you are entitled to know about our submersibles, too." The scientist hummed and hawed and seemed tortured, but then he finally spit it out. "The fact is that this complex you see all around us is only half of our project. There is a similar facility 4,500 miles west on the coast of Ecuador on the west coast of South America and, of course, we must stay in as close communication as possible. While we have successfully—through veiled buffer agencies—persuaded various governments that the establishment of a trans-Atlantic telegraph cable linking the two continents is vital,

And there it was, that marvelous gargantuan whale we had spied at the outset.

that link hasn't been completed quite yet. In the meantime, our urgent requirement for fast communication and transportation forced us to improvise."

Vividly aware of the huge diamond that was burning a hole in my pocket, I wasn't able to pay attention as I should have. Clearly Maxwell was frustrated that I didn't have more to say, so I forced myself to say something.

"Doctor, geography beyond southern Africa is not my forte, but I do seem to recall that Ecuador is on the other side of South America, that is on the Pacific side. If I stretch my imagination, I can conceive some sort of a cross-Atlantic communication line, but it's impossible to see how any cable or ship, no matter its shape, could easily move back and forth between Ecuador and Sierra Leone without being forced to navigate the Straits of Magellan at the bottom of South America."

"Oh, that is easy. We simply utilize the cross-Nicaragua underground river."

"The what? I don't understand," was all I could venture.

Maxwell said, "I can best explain by means of an illustration. Please step over here." We walked to a far corner of the room where there was a large table, and I only realized when we were right on top of it that the table top was a very large map. More specifically, it was a map of the Atlantic Ocean with South America on one side and Africa on the other side.

"Yes, that is exactly what it is. Now look at it closely. Do you see anything peculiar?"

I looked again and went over it with some exactness, but there was nothing that jumped out at me. When I delayed in responding, Maxwell said, "Look especially at the two coast lines."

I did and then I did see something. "The coasts almost look as though they could fit together, like two puzzle pieces."

"Yes, that is exactly what I hoped you would notice. Quatermain, there is in fact every reason to believe that in the distant past, the two coasts were connected, and that some unthinkably titanic convulsion millions upon millions of years ago split that landmass into two pieces and that the two continents have been drifting apart ever since."

That was the most wild and preposterous claim I had ever heard, and, being in a sour mood, I said as much, instantly being regretful of my outburst, but Maxwell went on probably because he didn't hear me in his enthusiasm.

"Well then," he continued, preening like a peacock, "let us go on to the next point. As you see, if there had been in the distant past a large deposit of a mineral, say silver, and whatever force split the landmasses happened to bisect that deposit of silver, then it stands to reason that if such a deposit was located today on the west coast of Africa, that one could find a comparable deposit along the northeast coast of South America."

Here he took a stick and pointed to the two areas just mentioned.

"As it happens," he continued, "the experiment we are performing here requires, in fact, two masses of silver that are some thousands of miles apart. We chose this location for our laboratory partly because of the proximity of one such silver mass (undiscovered to date of course and thank goodness or it wouldn't have lasted long). We sent some of our associates to South America to seek the other half of the silver lode in Brazil, but they were unable to isolate any such deposit, a fact we found perplexing. However, applying their geological and geographical knowledge, they did in fact find the deposit we were seeking in Ecuador."

"I still don't understand," said I.

"If we can agree that the two coasts seem to fit together like puzzle pieces, then here is another perspective that is not so obvious."

Here he pulled the continent of South America off the table (as it turns out that they were in fact pieces of a puzzle rather than a drawing as I had first supposed), and turned that continent 90 degrees and set the top of the continent adjacent to west Africa. I was amazed to see that this was an excellent fit as well!

"Thus you see that there are other possibilities," Maxwell continued. "This agreement of geography may well have preceded the more obvious one by some millions of years and it is this configuration which interests us."

Here he pointed his stick very deliberately. "You can see that Ecuador, then, would have abutted right up here to where we stand on the coast of Sierra Leone!"

※ ※ ※

When Maxwell had finished, I pondered his remarks and privately thought his thinking was flawed and that the whole thing was coincidence and it was preposterous for a noted scientist to take any of it seriously, but this time I kept my feelings to myself and merely nodded sagely. I don't recall now, but I may have also asked a few questions, enough to give him the impression that I understood what he was talking about.

"Thus," he went on, "just when it was becoming clear that we needed to somehow transport to and from, and to communicate with, the other laboratory 'over yonder,' which we would build in Ecuador, we began to cast about looking for a solution, and when we found it, it was two-fold! We found convincing evidence in a recently discovered document that a submersible had been built and was perfectly operational some two millennia ago. We also in the same document learned of the subterranean river under the southern portion of Central America that connects the Atlantic Ocean with the Pacific Ocean.

"But where did you get the plans? How could you even imagine that it was possible?"

"The solution came from an unexpected place," Maxwell said. "The British Museum, it seems, has a cache of codices and scrolls recovered from Ethiopia a few years ago, scrolls that had been saved from the Library of Alexandria sixteen hundred years ago."

I cannot adequately explain the degree of shock this man's words sent through me. In point of fact, Maria Mitchell and I had trekked in Ethiopia a year or two before. Well, in fact it was during that expedition that I had heard much about those self-same scrolls that had been rescued by Richard Holmes, the curator of the museum, who had accompanied Field-Marshal Napier during the 1868 Ethiopian campaign. But that is a wholly different adventure and needs to wait for another day. (Actually now that I think about it, I did already tell that story in the presence of two notable gentlemen in New York State of all places, shortly after I settled into the Grange. One of them, my friend Dr. Watson, took ample notes and, in fact wrote up the whole story and posted it to the other gentleman, the landscape painter Frederick Church.) [Editor's note: See The Great Detective at the Crucible of Life.]

Ah yes. I know John kept a copy—a copious thing, I fear. In any case, it was at this point that Maria turned to me there in the presence of Maxwell and Barbicane and winked, whispering, "Isn't it interesting how these things happen?"

I couldn't just let that go. "Maria, I distinctly remember that you used the word uncovered earlier! Uncovered indeed!"

She winked again. "I didn't think it was my place to tell you—and besides, I wanted to see your face when you were told."

Maxwell, meanwhile, ignoring our little tête-à-tête, was continuing: "The scrolls telling of the submarine boat described an astonishing design that incorporated great speed. That was our inspiration, and so we challenged Barbicane, who was well underway with the planning of both laboratories."

I exclaimed, "You mean to tell me that the Ecuadorian laboratory is as immense as this one with the same energy requirements?"

Here Maxwell looked meaningfully at Barbicane, who answered, "Yes. Pretty much insofar as it was necessary to dam the Sumatara and Chambo Rivers, and develop the same sort of reservoir and power complex, though it was somewhat simpler to build the gravity driven aqueduct system due to the rivers' descent down the Andes being significantly steeper compared to the equivalent descent from the Loma Mountains here." Here he vaguely pointed in the general direction of the mountains two hundred miles east of where we stood.

Then Barbicane cleared his throat and continued on the subject of submersibles, "When our sponsor, who had learned quickly of the British Museum's new Ethiopian acquisitions, approached us with a possible solution to our long-range transportation and communication problem, in the form of the two thousand-year-old papyrus scrolls, I was intrigued. And the part of my brain that is irrefutably an engineer began to spin plans instantly. But I had a second exceedingly important advantage that I had not consciously connected with our problem. You may remember, of course, that six or seven years ago, the newspapers were full of reports of sea monsters destroying ships—" He looked at me for affirmation, but I had none to give him.

I said, "Doctor, I haven't heard anything about sea monsters, and even if I had, I wouldn't have paid any attention!"

"But surely the furor—"

"I spend months at a time in back country. A hunting expedition to the Chobe River or my trading among the tribes of Nala and Wambe would have coincided with that time frame. It is not uncommon to be on safari for a year. Thus your furor may well have come and gone while I was trying to earn a living."

I admit I was a little put off by Barbicane's remark because I had become bored with the cosmopolitan style of the man who was assuming that everybody must know just what he knows and who can hardly fathom that there are some people whose livelihoods don't conveniently intersect with newspapers and magazines.

He went on, unfazed, "As I was saying, in any case, the United States government became determined to hunt the creatures down or know why not! The upshot is that accompanying the naval task force was a Professor

Aronnax, a French naturalist. Their mission had considerable success, though it was not the sort of discovery and resolution that the government could allow to be reported. Nevertheless, through mutual friends I was able to meet with Aronnax, and he described in detail the true nature of those so-called sea monsters. It turns out that there was only one of the creatures and that it wasn't a creature at all, but an armored submarine boat named *Nautilus* that was designed, built and commanded by one Captain Nemo. In the end, I pumped the professor for every scrap of information and data he could recount as it interested me immensely. Remember that our meeting was before the singular nature of the papyri scrolls had been discovered and, in fact, before our sponsor had any notion of what the future held for him. So, you see, I was the right man for the job. They had hired me in the first instance to build the laboratories. Building the *Nova* and the *Stella* was merely an adjunct to the larger project, but a most useful one. My principal contribution, I think, was the adaptation of the submersible's motive power from steam to stored electricity."

"*Stella!*" I had gulped, I remember, then cried forcibly. "You mean there are two of them?" (In truth, it was as difficult then as it is now to say that one special name aloud.)

"Certainly," Barbicane said. "Since we had all the infrastructure in place, the dry docks and so forth, it only made sense, and they have both been immensely useful. In fact, I have just returned from 'over yonder.' Everything is coming along fine, I'm happy to say!"

❊ ❊ ❊

Thus it stood for several weeks, our being housed pleasantly enough in the laboratory—though effectively against our will—though I, for Maria's sake, chose not to make an issue of the matter. After all, it was not as though Hans and I needed to be anywhere in particular and it was not as though our hosts were belligerent or indisposed overly much to our presence once they got used to our loitering around. They, however, quite ably diverted any suggestion or effort of mine to quit the place. (Well, I say that, but, of course, they would have given much to be rid of us; they simply didn't seem to have much of a choice; they were damned if they did and damned it they didn't.) And truth be told, I found that my curiosity had been piqued after I learned that the hoped for culmination of all this enormous work was expected in an unspecified "short time."

In fact, as can be imagined, I was torn. On one hand I truly enjoyed spending time with Maria. Though our backgrounds couldn't have been more different, I found I enjoyed the honest and straightforward interest she showed in Hans and me. I'd spent some time with her the year before, as I've said, and she certainly showed her intellectual side then, especially when propounding about the stars and comets, and I was affected then, as I was again in this instance, by her down to earth and straightforward and reliable manner.

But on the other hand, I had a fortune burning a hole in my pocket. That diamond was enormous and I have no doubt, looking back on it, that its value would have been far greater than the value of all the diamonds Sir Henry and John Good and I brought back from King Solomon's Mines, which have made us all wealthy, and my life so comfortable here in Britain in my new home, the Grange.

[One reason that I have not laid this story down before now is that I hesitated to impose onto the world yet another diamond story featuring the great Allan Quatermain, despite this adventure occurring a dozen years or so before I in fact became wealthy.]

Beyond my affection for Maria, I'd become interested and now I wanted to see how it all played out in the end. What could all this effort and material and money be for? Can you imagine the fortune all this must have cost—tens of thousands of workers, two two hundred-mile-long aqueducts, vast dam complexes arresting the flows of mighty rivers high in the mountains, power plants, and not one but two inconceivably large laboratories on opposite sides of the earth, the submersible boats—? Aside from the vague awareness that it all somehow had to do with learning something about the Star of Bethlehem, Hans and I knew nothing and we had no choice but to cool our heels.

The huge pits we had seen being dug on either side of the lab as we approached it had reached a sufficient degree of completion that the scaffolding had by now been dismantled and removed. The excavating equipment was removed, too, and it was then that I realized just exactly what the many plants with chimneys were producing—they were smelting silver, and the insides of the pits, or bowls, were being covered with silver leaf. Thousands of square yards of pure silver. In other words, while Hans and I loitered, we saw a vast fortune in silver coat those two fantastically huge bowls—and there were two others presumably just like them all the way over in Ecuador. The more I learned, the more preposterous it all became. A telescope indeed! I was not so stupid to be fooled so easily any further.

Eventually in the middle of the bowls grew arrangements of tubing and wires and scaffolding of a different sort and from which all manner of unfamiliar equipment was suspended, all shaped into a pattern I cannot begin to describe other than to say that it was complicated to the extreme.

✽ ✽ ✽

At any rate, it was now about eight weeks after we had arrived at the laboratory gates. Maria and Maxwell told me over breakfast that they were ready to calibrate the machine to, in effect, connect both laboratories and the vast machines that they had built—to create one inconceivable machine! I suspected that whatever happened next, it would not be dull.

Maxwell said, "We're going to begin adjusting our apparatus today. It may interest you, though I fear there will not be anything interesting to actually see. We will pull some levers and twist some knobs, and then the four units, two on either side of the world, will be connected for the first time via the submarine cable that the governments have only just finished laying on the floor of the Atlantic Ocean, and then we will have to calibrate for a few days."

So Maxwell and Maria led me back to the workshop. Typically, by the way, as it will be pertinent later on, by then Hans had got into the habit of removing himself each morning and I'd not see him again till the late afternoon. He didn't volunteer what he'd been up to, and if I asked, he declined to answer.

There was much more equipment in the room than the last time I'd been there. New shiny instruments had been neatly stacked on new racks that had been mounted onto the walls and new sturdy islands and tables had appeared mounded with still more equipment. I was led to the back of the room and we entered a dark alcove I'd not noted before, which was the case, I realized, because it had been screened off. Here there were two tables that seemed to be covered with toy buildings. But when lanterns had been ignited, what I saw reminded me of the table with the movable puzzle pieces by which Maxwell had explained the positioning of the continents. These tables were on either side of the room. The one on the right side of the room, closest to me, held not toys, but a model. It was obviously a representation of the very laboratory where we'd been honored guests all those weeks. It was a tiny reproduction of the main points of the facility, or town—the temple, the buildings, the trains and tracks, the aqueduct and power stations, and the two huge bowls that we'd only just seen completed.

After I had oriented myself to the model, Maxwell led me across the room to another table with a similar model.

"This is the laboratory in Ecuador. As you see, its general makeup is similar to ours. We simply call it 'over yonder' usually."

And it was so. A small town with its own array of tracks—with two perfectly equivalent bowls!

"Now step back, Quatermain, and view the set up from that raised platform."

I did so and took in the sight before me. It certainly was impressive. I knew that the space between them represented both the Atlantic Ocean and the whole breadth of the South American continent.

I said, "And with this you will listen to the mind of God?"

And then I heard an unfamiliar voice. It said in English with an Italian accent, "Yes, that is our hope."

I looked down toward the voice that had surprised me, and there stood a Roman Catholic priest, which was obvious from his collar. I climbed down from the platform and greeted the man.

Barbicane, who happened to enter just then made the introductions. "Quatermain, this is His Eminence, Alberto Cardinal Cigliutti, Prefect of the Holy Office and Vatican Secretary of State. Under the circumstances, his boss, as you can imagine, has a vested interest in our little experiment, and he is here as an observer."

I shook the cardinal's hand and muttered something about an expensive toy, and he responded naturally enough, when I think back on it, "My dear Quatermain, I suppose you are speaking ironically or sarcastically. I can't tell which because my English is not up to such subtleties. Regardless, this attempt to glean something fundamental of the Almighty is one of the greatest works projects since the building of the Suez Canal, which pales by comparison. And it is infinitely more important, as the canal merely makes passage easier between west and east, whereas our goal is to receive the will of the creator of all the universe!"

I said something polite and turned to Barbicane and asked when the show would be on the road. What followed was exactly as Maxwell had predicted. Knobs were turned and levers pulled and orders recorded. To be polite, I hung around for a couple of hours and then retired to the hotel and took a nap.

Here there were two tables that seemed to be covered with toy buildings.

Thus it stood for a few days. Maria, Maxwell, Barbicane, and I would breakfast, then Maria and Maxwell would go straight to the workshop. Though Barbicane inevitably wound up there before long, he would always go elsewhere on inspection tours upon leaving the table.

Then one day I noticed that the hair all over my body had begun to tingle and stand up. Plus there was an unaccountable faint rushing sound in the air like running water that seemed to emanate from everywhere. It was both frightening and distinctly uncomfortable. Soon after I noticed this, I received a message that I was needed in the workshop. Hans, as usual, was nowhere to be found, and I went alone.

Maria met me at the door, clearly very excited. "Allan! All is ready! You're just in time. We need you now to please be a witness. Sh-h-h, James is going to speak." I saw that he and Barbicane and Cigliutti were standing at a chalk board at the front of the room.

"Everybody!" Maxwell called out. I should say that the room had somehow managed to squeeze in perhaps one hundred scientists and technicians, most of who were talking and comparing notes.

"Everybody!" They all finally quieted down and Maxwell continued, "The moment has arrived! We've all been working against the clock on an impossible deadline, and we have succeeded beyond our wildest dreams. On both sides of this planet earth we are pointing our telescope toward the constellation Aquila. The power that we harnessed is coursing through all the materials that surround us. Whatever happens next, we will be a better people for it!"

That was all. He stepped over to some equipment and turned a knob. Immediately, everyone in the room began their tasks, including Maria, who had a device over her ears and was listening intently, pad and pencil in hand. The next thing I knew, an array of tubes was flashing and sparks were flying everywhere. There were spinning wheels large and small. Switches were pulled and pushed, and meters and dials were moving like fury. The tingling and buzz that I'd been aware of all day intensified, frighteningly so.

Frankly, I felt more in the way than anything else, but Maria had told me that I was needed, so I remained.

Maxwell was on the raised platform. Cigliutti was next to him. Maxwell began screaming commands. It was controlled pandemonium for perhaps ten minutes.

And then it all stopped, and all was quiet.

Without being told, I knew that something had gone wrong. The room had grown hot and there was an air of disappointment. Maxwell didn't look happy. "All right gentlemen, we will recalibrate and try again in an hour!"

And what I have just described was repeated half a dozen times through the day and the disappointment turned to despondency. But they soldiered on and recalibrated again and again. In time, at nightfall, exhausted, Maxwell announced that they would stop and rest—rather than work—for thirty minutes before continuing.

🌿 🌿 🌿

It was towards the end of this respite that Hans finally appeared at my side. "Hans, where have you been? History is being made—I think."

"Well, Baas, if history has to do with spooks, then I have much to tell you. O, Baas! This day I've been haunted by more spooks than—"

But he was cut off, as Maxwell called out. Again, electricity flowed through the whole room, and sparks again flew and containers containing colored liquid began to gurgle and bubble furiously. Hans, despite his endless worldly posing, was clearly in awe of that show of exotic energy.

You could feel the tension increase, and this time the mood in the room swung over to joy.

Slowly, a peculiar steady hissing hum could be heard and soon overwhelmed all the mechanical sounds combined. It was a steady hiss that increased in volume. All the while Hans' eyes opened wider and wider (as mine must have also, truth to tell) and then, suddenly, I felt Hans' body jerk to attention. He seemed absolutely riveted. If it had been a momentary thing, I wouldn't have worried, as such shocks happen all the time—usually a tingling in the spine or a chill—but my concern increased as his eyes grew wider and as he stood thus longer and longer, and then his mouth began to open and close and his lips moved as though he was forming words, mainly without sound—but intermittently he vocalized some clicks that are part of his Hottentot language. I said something to him, but he was able to distinctly communicate "no," by words or change in posture I don't know, but I understood that I ought not interrupt.

Maxwell and the others were clearly riveted as well by the constant hiss that filled the room. I haven't mentioned it yet, but the room was filled with stenographers, listening to every word spoken by every soul in there and recording every one of those words-—Hans and me, too, for all I knew. Indeed, there were machines with pens that recorded all the other sounds, and they were responding wildly to the hum or hiss or whatever it was. I was worried about poor Hans, whose body had snapped to attention and stayed thus for nearly a half hour. But suddenly his body relaxed and folded, and he would have collapsed onto the floor if I hadn't caught him and quietly carried him out of the room.

Once we were outside and Hans was steady on his feet, I said, "What on earth happened to you in there? It looked like you were hit by lightening!" A simple enough observation and question, I suppose, and here is the gist of his response.

"Baas! Baas! You will not believe! I've seen and heard your Predikant father, and while I did in fact see him, the conversation was all on his side and thus I mainly heard him."

Hans was always making the most ridiculous pronouncements; especially having to do with things he could know nothing about—statements rife with superstition.

"What is it, Hans? What do you mean? I'll admit that you seem more pale under that yellow skin of yours!"

"O, Baas, you don't know the half of it."

"What do you mean that you saw my father, the Predikant, and that he spoke to you?"

"Baas, I am easily bored by all the chatter that I don't understand and it hurts my head and that is why I always go off somewhere in the mornings. Well, Baas, as you know, they have here a sort of general store and the folk who tend the store are much like you, Baas, and are very neat and take the garbage out to bins during the day. Well, this morning I chanced to be in the area when I noticed that the door had not been fully closed the last time the garbage went out. Out of curiosity, I peered through the slight space between the door and its jamb, and lo! What do I see but a case full of square-face. Your Predikant father will scold me, I'm sure when I reach the Place of Fires, but I could not help myself nor could I control my hand as it squeezed between the door and its jamb of its own accord and grabbed two bottles. I told my hand and arm that they had sinned but that didn't stop them from uncorking the bottles."

"Hans, you silly fool, stop the speech. You are trying to tell me that you stole a couple of bottles of gin and got drunk."

"Yes, that is it exactly, Baas."

My thought was to shrug off this admission, as it was hardly the first time Hans had transgressed the rules of life as laid down by my father.

"Yes, Baas, but this time it was far more than that. First of all, as I was getting drunk, I felt very guilty—far more guilty than I have ever felt before while stealing square-face and getting drunk and sinning before the spirit of your Predikant father who I served so faithfully since you were a boy, Baas!

"One other thing, Baas, as I slept this morning, I dreamed of that pretty but evil diamond that I found in the temple pool. Do you remember that diamond, Baas? Do you remember who found that diamond and nearly drowned for the sake of that pretty stone? Thus, while you still slept, O, Macumazana!, I took the stone that you always keep wrapped with paper and string from your pocket where you always keep it so that it won't get lost, and I substituted an ordinary stone also in paper and string."

"O, no, Hans, don't tell me you lost it!"

"O, no, yourself, Baas. No, I didn't lose it. But, of course, my guilt was doubled now because I had two thefts on my conscience and was drunk besides and knew full well that your Predikant father was looking up at me from the Place of Fires and that he frowned very sadly as he did so. As all this is going through my mind, I wandered over to the temple because the falling water and rising spray and thunderous roar always seem to relax my mind, and because of my great guilt, I very much needed to calm my head down."

Now I knew precisely what Hans was saying because I have myself felt a special tranquility when I have been at the temple, and, as such, I was sometimes drawn to it myself unaccountably.

He continued: "As soon as I got there, Baas, everything changed. The sun that had been hot and bright went behind a cloud and all became dark and cold. I shivered and my knees felt weak and I sat down on the marble floor with my back to the well and pulled my knees up to my chest and huddled up to myself."

Hans then paused in his story and looked inquisitively up to the skies, probably toward the Heaven that my father taught him about, and also toward the ground, where many Africans—including Hans' Hottentot forebears, of course, believe their afterlife will be played out—in the "Place of Fires."

As I was saying, Hans paused and then he said, "Now here it becomes confusing, Baas. I probably fell to sleep, but I cannot say for sure. Well I remember the sudden cold and my shivering, and I looked over toward the forest edge and I saw something sparkle. At first I thought it looked like a cloud of embers. Then I realized that it was a cloud of embers, and I thought I saw someone step out of the burning cloud. Then I was afraid because I realized that people don't step out of embers and then I knew that it was a spook. I was still cold and didn't want to see the spook, and so I closed my eyes. I think they were closed for a long time, but, of course, after a time I had to open them. I saw that the cloud of embers was still there and that the figure that had been emerging from it had not moved from where I first saw it, but now that I'd opened my eyes, it began to walk toward me, neither slow nor fast and I knew right away who it was, Baas. It was your Reverend Predikant father."

"You were drunk, Hans."

"Perhaps you are right, Baas. So in that case I saw your father while I was drunk. But he was a spook, I'm sure, just the same, Baas. Now, you know how much I hate spooks, even if they disguise themselves as your Predikant father. So I shut my eyes once more and covered my face with my hands, and put my head between my knees, and rolled over on my side and faced toward the well wall."

"Well," Hans continued, "eventually I opened my eyes and looked to see your father still walking toward me, but by then I'd learned that pretending it didn't exist did no good, so I decided to watch and wait. That it was your father, or perhaps a spook who did a good job of seeming to be your father, I had no doubt. In time, he stopped right in front of me and patiently waited for me to pay attention. Finally, I was able to say something."

"What did you say to him?"

"I said to your Predikant father, 'Whoa, Baas! Why are you here? What do you want of me?' And he said, 'Hans, my old friend, do not be scared. I need you to do one or two things for me.'

"'Ask me anything, O, father of Macumazana,' I said, "'and you know I will try,' and he said right back, 'The first thing I need you to do is remember. It is important to remember everything that you will see and hear and feel this day and convey it to my son.'"

"What did he mean, 'the first thing'?"

"I will get to that soon, Baas. There is much more to tell you."

"Hans, why on earth would my father choose to make himself manifest to an old drunken Hottentot like you, rather than to his own son, if anything you say is true?"

"I don't know Baas, except you know I loved him and he loved me and charged me to take care of you for as long as I lived, a charge I have happily and faithfully fulfilled to this day, and I hope many more, because I care for you as I cared for him, and as you care for me—though you would never say so to me—though mayhap some day when I am no longer here, you will tell anyone who will listen."

"Is there more, Hans?"

"Yes, Baas. Even as I looked, the embers washed over him and in a minute he was covered with them and, in another minute, both he and the embers began to fade, and then they were all gone, and it was as though none of it had ever happened, and I was left wondering if I had dreamed the whole thing. Except that I was still cold and shivered, and I had not moved from my huddled position, and so I knew that it had happened, and right now I am this very moment doing just as your Predikant father required of me: I am remembering and telling you about all that happened at the temple well."

He was nearly panting due to the struggle of telling me all this. I asked, "And all the while, you were clutching the diamond?"

"O, yes, Baas. Never for a second did my fingers loosen from around that pretty stone."

"That pretty stone, as you call it, Hans, will make us both more wealthy than it is possible to imagine."

"Yes, Baas, of course it will. But you should know some other things." Here he gulped and looked all around as though startled. Recall that after Hans' legs had given out from under him, I had led him outside and behind the laboratory building.

"I closed my eyes again, Baas, for a long time, and then opened them half expecting your Predikant father to be standing there again, but, of course, he, or rather, his spook, was gone. Then there was silence for a time. It seemed a long time, and then another voice, a new voice laughed loudly, or rather, an old voice as we both know it well. It said, 'Hans, you yellow dog, attend me!' It said again, 'Hans, attend me!' And then I understood that this new voice was the Great One." That is to say, the wizard Zikali, also known as "the Opener of Roads."

"'What is it that you want, you old devil?' I cried, knowing perfectly well that he was even then squatting in his hut, as he hates to travel in the flesh because he finds it so much more convenient to let his spirit fly. The voice said, 'I am here with you, as real as if you were standing next to my hut.'

"'So what? You say this, but why should I believe you, as the Baas always tells me that you are nothing but an old cheat? I'm probably hearing things due to my having been thinking a lot about square-face and also drinking it.'

"'Stop yammering, little yellow man, and attend me!'

"This seemed a simple enough thing to do and the wisest course of action, so I did not argue. As you know, when dealing with the Great One,

one's first response is to run the other direction because he is so ugly, also so powerful, also for fear he might 'sniff' you out."

"What do you fear being sniffed out about, Hans?"

"Baas, you know that I have my follies as does every man, though some men (and women too) have more follies and therefore are more fools than others and therefore may be prone to seizures of guilt, and I cannot deny that I have done many things in my dirty and slothful life that I'm not proud of. In any case, I determined to merely do as Zikali asked, or rather ordered!

"'Listen to me, you fool!' he droned on. 'When next you see Macumazana, be sure that you pay attention and listen to everything that you hear all around both of you. Listen to the very air itself! Listen and be surprised! Listen and become wise. Be most careful and listen with your ears and listen with you heart! And then when all is done, tell Macumazana all that you heard and all that you saw.' He seemed more than usually mean and angry, Baas.

"Then, Baas, it must have been that I sleepwalked. I soon realized that I was no longer at the temple anymore, but that I had somehow got into one of those long tunnels that connect the big bowls with the laboratory buildings. And then I heard the voice of your Predikant father again, Baas. I could not see him, but it was his voice all the same."

"What did my father say this time to you, Hans?"

"He said, 'Something more, Hans: Hide the stone! Now, Hans, hide the stone in the tunnel. It's important! Trust me, Hans!' Of course, I did not trust my senses, but no sooner than I heard him say this I heard someone enter the tunnel from the opposite end, and so I quickly found a box on the wall and shoved the diamond into it to hide."

"God in heaven! Do you mean our diamond is stashed in a box in plain sight of the technicians who fill that service corridor night and day and who are even now trying to repair the machine?"

"That's about the size of it!"

I was so angry at Hans I could have wrung his skinny neck right there. I wanted to go to the tunnel right then and there, but Hans took my arm and held me back.

"But wait, Baas, I, that is we, are not nearly done. There is more! So much more. And I have promised the spooks that I would tell you all!"

He stopped and seemed to gather his thoughts for a minute, and I waited.

"So then I escaped unseen," he continued, "and waited for the corridor to clear out so I could retrieve the stone, which I had hid for no better reason than the command of a spook who sounded like your Reverend Predikant father. I hid for a while but the tunnel was always full of men, thus I came looking for you."

"And when you found me, you promptly passed out!"

"Not at first, Baas. Much happened before I became so weak and would have hit the floor if you had not caught me. Remember, Baas, that just as I walked into the room, all the Baases with the beards and their servants and, too, the star lady of whom we are both so fond, were growing happy even as I came in, or they seemed relieved like a great boulder had flown right off their shoulders. Remember that I had just joined you and that we were standing there in that big room with the lightning that jumped off the walls like fleas. And as we watched it all, there came a sound—a sort of hissing sound from out of the lightning—that began quietly and soon filled the room, and it seemed that it was this sound that made all the Baases so happy. You saw! After standing shocked for a minute, with their eyes bugging out, they all got busy again, even more so than they usually are, and as they did things the sound changed, quieter, then louder, then almost shrieking, then a whisper."

Frankly I was amazed that Hans had noticed so much—far more than I, who was mainly irritated by the whole proceedings. Nevertheless, it was just as he described, now that he called it to my attention.

"Yes, Hans, all those things happened. What is so important that you must tell me now, even before we go fetch the diamond?"

"Baas, just this! As that hissing sound began I began to hear a faint voice, a small voice, like a small cat caught behind a cupboard door on the other side of the house. It seemed far distant and so low, but it was accompanied by a quiet drawn-out drumming sound. I could hear the voice, the drumming, and the hissing all at once."

"I tell you, you were drunk, Hans."

"No, or rather yes! But not like this have I ever been drunk, Baas. The distant voice said, or rather whispered because it was so low and almost drowned out by the other sounds, the most strange thing. It said it was the holy trumpet announcing, heralding, the most divine voice yet to come and I was drunk because it, the trumpet, had made me get drunk, and that it wanted me to be drunk, the better to hear with. And no sooner did I understand this, than the voice just disappeared altogether like when you think you might be hearing something in the distance, but then the wind changes direction and it is gone and you are left not knowing if you heard anything at all."

"What did the voice you might have heard want you to hear, Hans?" I couldn't believe that I was asking such an inane question! But when no reply was forthcoming, I asked, "And everything you've said about this strange voice was something you heard—through your ears—and nothing that you saw?"

I don't know what made me ask a question with such a self-evident answer, but Hans responded, "Good question, Baas. I don't know. It almost felt as though I was hearing it through my skin. And then, as I said, it was gone."

"Where is all this leading, Hans?" I asked, my temper growing short.

"Only this, Baas! Ha! All those silly fools with all their machines and whale-boats and brains were trying to hear some sort of message from the Great Baas in the sky. They told us so! Well, they succeeded, but they did not recognize it and will never do so! Yet I, Hans, poor yellow dog drunken Hans, heard the Great Baas' voice and it spoke to him."

"What on earth are you talking about, Hans?"

"Only this, after the small voice that said I was supposed to be drunk came and went, I could hear the hissing more clearly, and I paid attention. At first it was low, but then it became louder and terrible like a room full of snakes, and then the hissing changed and became the flapping of giant wings—just like great wings—and then I thought I could hear words coming from somewhere, but I couldn't make out where they were coming from, but finally I understood that the voice was the hissing sound! I was amazed and at first forgot that I was supposed to remember everything that happened. You will not believe me, Baas, but I swear on your Reverend father's grave that it is true. The hissing sound that filled the room, mixed with popping and crackling sounds, was speaking to me in my own Hottentot click language! O, how I wished then that I could claim to be more drunk than I was. I became scared—very, very frightened, as scared as I have ever been—and then the fear died and I began to feel like I do sometimes when we have reached the top of a tall hill and there is a great green valley below us, or a raging ocean blown around by a storm. What I felt, Baas, was this: It was like a great claw was scraping and tearing at my soul, the very soul your Reverend Predikant father was always telling us about, but I was not so much afraid of it or even hurt by it as I was full of curiosity about what it was and I ached in other ways, not with pain and hurt as you would expect great talons to do, but I ached with yearning to know more. But of course it wasn't really a claw, I just said it felt like one."

"Hans, this story is indeed much different from your normal run of excuses for getting drunk, but I am losing interest. If you have a reason for

"I, Hans, heard the Great Baas' voice and it spoke to him."

this story, you had better tell me now."

"Just this, Baas. As I said, the hissing spoke to me in my own click language. The voice came through clearly and spoke at length and gave me a message, and it repeated the message several times so I would remember it forever, and once I had memorized it, the language of my fathers faded and changed and again became mere scratching and gibberish."

"Well, Hans, are you going to take all day? Give me the message if you really have a message to give me."

And this is what Hans told me those many years ago:

"'O, Hans the good!'

"Yes, Baas, that is what the voice said to this old yellow monkey, as the Great One usually enjoys calling me.

"'Hans the mischievous. Hans the child. Hans the wise. I wish you to be the vessel of my message to all the people.'

"Here, Baas, despite being haunted by spooks for half the day, I was more surprised to be spoken to by the lightning, or rather by the clicks buried in the lightning, and I responded, 'Great Baas, as you must be or you wouldn't be speaking to me thus. Why are you playing with my head? Leave me alone.'"

"Hans," I said, "I was watching you and I did see your lips move, but it was some time later that you spoke out loud."

"I don't know what to tell you, Baas. I'm only saying what I know, and what I was told I was supposed to repeat back to you."

Chastened, I said, "What else did this voice say to you?"

"Only this, Baas: 'Hans, your fathers and their fathers and their fathers, and also all the mothers, all the way back to the dawn of time, have watched the stars and the sun and the moon move across the sky. Also, your people and all peoples have noted that sometimes the moon will precisely cover the sun, and the light and warmth will vanish! Can anything be more frightening? I ask.

"'Listen, Hans the faithful! Perhaps fear of hunger or of cold or of enemies or of pain or of death can be as frightening. But these are all things that are part of life and are expected, thus assumed, and though they may be feared, they are not strange. For does not every man fully expect his lot to be touched by these fearsome things at some point during his journey?

" 'However, the greatest joy in a person's life, indeed, in a whole people's life, is warmth and light from the sun. Thus the fear that comes from the sun vanishing and the world growing dark is the most fearsome thing of all for there is no way of knowing when such a terrible thing will happen. It is not like the sun setting and rising.

" 'Or at least this was so up until the various peoples discovered by their industry my secret pattern. Man, i.e., humans or humankind, has become fully human because he sought to know when in the future the circle of the moon would cover the circle of the sun and plunge the earth into darkness. Behold! In time, each people built tools and discovered the pattern in the randomness. They learned when the fearsome thing would occur, and they became less afraid. They found the secret that I had buried deep within the complexities I'd created just to goad humans to seek it.

" 'I tell you that humankind's seeking to predict when the moon will cover the sun is what has made humans human. This is the key that honed problem solving far beyond that needed for mere survival. From this has sprung all that makes humans human.

" 'Thus peoples built grand temples and pyramids and statues and standing stones to observe the sun and moon and sky, and, sometimes, they enslaved whole peoples to build their observatories. Hans, this took many thousands of years, during which time people have done much for both good and ill. But remember that it all began due to fear of losing the sun during the day—a fear I instilled by making certain that the moon exactly covers the sun. I created a problem that humankind needed to solve and thereby progress!

" 'Surely nowadays many people have studied that age-old problem and have for centuries grown to understand thoroughly the remote—I say again—remote probability of any such equality in size of the sun and moon, so small a probability that the fact of this equivalence is on the surface preposterous. Yet, too often people just shrug and call it coincidence. Too few reach the next logical conclusion. If such a thing is preposterous, and yet exists nonetheless as a fact of life, what could it mean? Perhaps it means that someone wished it all to happen in just that manner. But who could wish up suns and moons and propel human advancement?

" 'Who indeed? Humans now have clear reason to know me. I am right there in the maths and calculations that they treasure so much, but they can also be stubborn, can take things terribly for granted and rationalize. Still, Hans, people will someday understand that something is happening, has always been happening, that defies reason, yet has a cause and that cause is me—for I am that I am!

"'But first there must come a drawn-out time when the blind will lead and these words I am saying will verily be the light in the darkness. Old Hans, share my words. Remember all that I've said and share it with your Baas, Allan, O Hans the child, Hans the wise!

"'For you are my messenger.'"

While at the time, I honestly feared for Hans, years later when I happened to think upon the odd words of his soliloquy, a memory came with a shock, an electric shock, an eerie shock that shook me to my soul—because just such an eclipse as Hans described in principle saved me and Sir Henry and John Good from serious trouble during our adventure to King Solomon's Mines. We had got in trouble with the Kukuanas in that region and would have certainly been slaughtered had not Good remembered a notation he'd glimpsed in the almanac that he always carried with him. That almanac identified that the following day at one o'clock there would commence a total eclipse of the sun. Well, we there and then claimed to be great wizards with mighty powers and declared that we would extinguish the sun to prove it. We succeeded in creating doubt, sufficient to postpone our executions, and sure enough, the solar eclipse happened right on schedule, with all the resultant reactions in the native mind that Hans had listed out. [Publisher's note: At the "37th thousand printing" of King Solomon's Mines, someone—an editor? a publisher?—changed all references and descriptions in the book of this solar eclipse to that of a Lunar eclipse!] But I won't go into any further detail now as that adventure was the first that I wrote up—even before I retired to come here—and my agent thinks it will likely be publishable before long.

Well, getting back to what I was saying, no sooner had Hans divested himself of all this nonsense, than he scampered off as he was wont to do. Naturally, I hurried to the service corridor he spoke of and loitered for ages waiting for the place to clear out so I could fetch the diamond that Hans said my father had told him to hide there. I could just see into the tunnel from where I stood and I spotted the box mounted on the wall perhaps fifty feet from the entrance. Before long, the corridor didn't clear out so much as there was a chance moment when perhaps a dozen stressed, sweating, coughing individuals had gone their separate ways, and for a brief time the spot I needed was accessible! I ran in and made a beeline to the box, opened it, and, to my delight, found the paper-wrapped stone, pulled it out and thrust it into my pocket, and only then did I feel in a position to breathe again, ever since Hans began to tell me his ghost story, as I suppose you would call it.

There isn't much more to tell. Hans and I had stumbled onto a most strange enterprise, become reacquainted with an old friend, had been detained against our wills, spent time with some notable scientists and engineers, and observed with our own eyes the expenditure of uncounted millions to build enormous pieces of equipment the like of which I can never adequately describe let alone understand in terms of purpose.

All I can say for sure is that Hans believed to the day that he died that he had touched something divine, or rather that something had touched him, and he felt satisfied that he had conveyed to me that which he had been ordered to memorize and convey back to me, but what of it? What would I do with such irredeemable nonsense? Except forget it—as I have in fact done until now, and in fact, it makes my heart sore to remember Hans at such a low ebb. It was likely some sort of trick perpetrated by Zikali just to prove a point—of what I can't imagine—though in later days, he denied any direct involvement. Of course, he knew all about everything that Hans claimed to have experienced, as he is prone to do with anything that is remotely mysterious.

I'm close to the end. Poor Maxwell and Barbicane and Cardinal Cigliutti tried over and again to receive some sort of signal from the star in the constellation Aquila, and never heard or measured anything of consequence more than that continuous hiss that I've described. Hans and I remained there for a week further to keep Maria company, but in the end, it was clear that their expensive toy was a failure and that nothing could come of fine-tuning their instruments any further. Heartbroken that all their immense effort, manpower, and expense to hear some whisper from God about the divinity of His son was for naught, they rallied and began to make plans to destroy it all.

Barbicane suggested to me that Hans and I should leave quickly and be well on our way at the end of twenty-four hours because they had no choice but to erase the laboratory from existence. He did not elaborate, but I could tell he was deadly serious. One wonders what the fate of it all would have been if the experiment had been a success. Certainly I'll never know.

I sought out Maria, and we said farewell, which was of course sad, but I was glad to be on my way finally, and she was clearly happy to be returning to her former life as a professor of astronomy in America. She told me that she and Maxwell and the rest would be boarding a British naval vessel and be leaving before dawn. She told me that they were left with immense amounts of data of an unknown sort, and that she would remain in touch with Maxwell, and perhaps they would be able to extract something of scientific value from the whole experience.

The next morning, from the top of the same hill from which we first saw the town, as we thought of it then, but which we came to know as an unprecedentedly prodigious laboratory, we spied a ghost town. In the distance out over the ocean was a great naval ship in full sail and moving rapidly toward the horizon.

Then in an instant, the whole facility exploded. With heaven knows how much dynamite—I suppose it must have been dynamite, which was new and controversial then—they destroyed everything they had labored so hard to build. Even the temple that had captured our hearts from the start vanished, as well the incredible aqueduct that fed into it, and presumably all the dams and reservoirs, too, high up in the mountains. It all jumped into the air in fire and smoke that rose without let-up. Hans and I watched for a time, having very mixed emotions. When the smoke cleared, we saw that some structures had escaped the brunt of the blast, and we could still make out clearly the two bowls on either side of the make-shift town. Of course, I suppose all that silver leaf with which they had covered the bowls must have been stripped away and carted off. In the years since then I've heard rumors of huge pits and ruined buildings being swallowed by the jungle in that region, thus I conclude they never did finish the clean-up and erasure of their occupation. With regard to the two submersible boats, of which Hans and I saw only one, the *Nova*, we never set eyes on it again, and I simply have no idea what became of them. I would think that they'd be too valuable to scuttle outright, but, as I said, I just don't know. Likewise, I never learned or heard anything more about an equivalent base of operations in Ecuador, not that I was ever in a position to banter with those who would know about anything of the sort in South America!

As we turned to leave and descend the hill, Hans said, "Baas, somewhere in this very strange tale there must be a lesson similar to the sort of thing that your Predikant father used to drum into the heads of all the poor workers and students, of which sometimes I was counted."

"If so, Hans, I'm at a loss to see it. The whole affair seems to have been a detour with little enough value."

"Well, then, if you, Baas, the wise Macumazana, can find no meaning in any of this, then I say curse it all!"

And thereupon, he vented his anger and frustration by cursing just about everything.

"Curse this hill and that great fish. Curse the natives that told you of the white witch doctors. Curse the white witch doctors and all their machines. Curse the temple and the river that ran to it and the mountains from which it was born and curse the rain that fell on the mountains and made the river. Curse that hen's egg of a stone that the river brought down for me to find. Curse me for finding it. Curse its pretty shininess that tempted me so. Curse Zikali for knowing full well what would befall us as he always knows such things. And curse you, Baas, for getting us into this mess to begin with."

By now Hans was breathless and his eyes were red and bulging and I decided it was time for me to step in and calm my servant down. But he wasn't quite done, after all.

"And curse the noise from the sky in which I heard voices, and curse the voices, and curse me for hearing the voices!"

🌿 🌿 🌿

Then our life regained some of its normalcy. I decided that I had seen more of West Africa than I cared to and decided not to go back north to catch a ship back to Durban. We hired some porters, reequipped ourselves with oxen and wagons and trekked southeast to see what trading situations I could set up and also to hire myself out as the hunter that was my chief occupation then.

Some months later, Hans and I found ourselves on the outskirts of Zululand, and over a fire we chatted about the sundry challenges we had overcome that day because any day in the rough country of Africa is tantamount to a test of endurance. While we sat thus, in time I became absorbed by the flickering wood fire and simply stared into it, when Hans voiced the very subject that was really on my mind.

"How will you spend the money you will fetch from the great stone that I found, Baas?"

Well, I began by mentioning a certain mansion that had come onto the market in Pretoria after its then owner—an officer in the Army had perished in battle—I know not how. Having no wife or other heirs to speak of, his executors had put the property up for sale a year before, and so far as I knew there had been no takers, as apparently the asking price was exorbitant by any standards. So I fantasized in my response to Hans that I intended to march into the responsible agent's office and state that I wished to purchase the house at its current price, and oh, by the way, here is cash on the barrelhead, and a gratuity besides!

"And then, you Hans," I said, "can be head servant and the whole world will be at our beck and call!"

Of course, Hans saw through my weakness and my dreams of avarice.

"Baas, forgive me if your humble servant disagrees with you, but I don't understand why you are happy by such a future. I think you are better off giving the pretty stone back to the earth gods, for they will doubtlessly be very unhappy when they discover that their plaything is missing, and they will track us down and cause us much grief. May your Predikant father forgive me for speaking of such forbidden gods, but still I think we will not hear the end of their anger and our lives will be less than worthless in time—even in the big house that you dream of! Friends you never knew you had will hound you. Offspring that I never knew I had will likewise cause me no end of trouble. And what is the use of being head servant when all the servants will be forever plotting against me and sneaking their filthy hands into my pockets, as you, too, will find out—but the hands you will fight off will be the bigger hands of bigger men, even men with six and eight hands, like insects, and moving so fast that you will never know that they emptied your pockets until it is too late—and then we will regret that we ever carried that cursed stone away from the place where we found it!"

Hans was clearly in one of his lecturing moods, which he slipped into whenever he thought he was wiser than either my father or me, so I just let him have his tirade, after which I figured I would give him a drop of gin or not depending on my mood. I forget what I did then.

A few days later we were crossing the Mambuzo River. The sun was straight overhead. I remember that it was a crisp beautiful day and that I didn't mind one bit that I was soaked up to my chest due to the necessity of crossing the river. And, then, on impulse, I reached into my jacket pocket where I had kept the diamond all along and pulled it out. I unwrapped the soaked paper that was covering it and discreetly held it up to the sun and squinted as the sun's rays penetrated its magical substance. But I knew then that the sun's rays were harsh and were never intended for men to stare into for long. Then I clenched the diamond in the fist of my hand, swung my arm around a few times to limber up and hurled the stone into the deepest part of the river as far from me as I could.

Hans, who notices everything, looked at me with eyes as big as saucepans and his jaw dropped.

"Baas…Baas…"

"Quiet fool," I countered, "can't you see that I decided that your wisdom won the day."

We were both standing in the middle of the river. The water was up to his chin, as he was so much shorter than me (imagine me talking of comparative heights!). Behind us were two wagons and on the shore in front of us, our other two wagons had already been secured. A dozen porters were all around us, half drowned as we all were, but they were ignorant of the little drama that was being played out between Hans and myself.

"But, Baas, you threw away your big house and the servants that I would boss around!"

"Yes, I did, Hans." I glared at him and we thenceforth did not talk about it again.

Now that this whole affair has been recorded, I can still say that my mind has never been able to grasp any part of it either, despite Hans and I being in the middle of it all. Still, here I sit a wealthy man as the result of finding untold riches in diamonds. It seems I was fated to experience all these trappings and much of the downside, as well, just as poor dear old Hans predicted, for good or ill I don't know yet!

Thus, here I am at the end of this account and I wish my last words recorded here to be: I sorely miss Hans! O, how I hope, as I so often pray mantra-like to myself, I hope I do find the light of his love burning like a beacon in the darkness as he promised I should do, and that it may guide and warm my shivering new-born soul before I dare the adventure of the Infinite. O, I've been so lost without him!

THE END

THE SECRET CITY

Our story tells of the lengths mand and chruch would go to explain a two-millenia-old Mystery. The setting of the novel is a Top Secret Laboratory on the coast of Sierra Leone. Througout, it's imlied that the lab's infrastructure is so astoundingly immense it can only be inferred. Here was my chance to show what is behind the curatin. It goes into sme detail about the magnitude of the project and the infrastructure at its center. Another thread ruminates on the effect on humanity of total solar eclipses and their implications; the startling import of these eclipses.

THOMAS KENT MILLER – My interests include science-fiction movies, Victorian and Edwardian ghost stories, 19th-century Hudson River School landscape paintings, and home theater. I also have an interest in Sherlock Holmes and have written some fiction that includes that Great Detective. I have university degrees in Journalism and Creative Writing, and live in southern California.

I have been gratified by some recent publishing successes aside from Airship 27's publishing this novella, The Star of Wonder. For decades I've been trying to get people to take notice of the 1980 masterpiece of cosmic haunting, Thomas Bontly's Celestial Chess, originally published by Harper and Row. As fate would have it, an academic friend recently mentioned this to the Bruin Books publisher, with the end result that a beautiful 40th Anniversary edition was published November 2019, and I was honored to be asked to provide a new introduction.

Since 1973, when I read H. Rider Haggard's The People of the Mist, he's been one of my two favorite authors, to the degree that I've written four Haggard pastiche novels. My other favorite is Arthur Machen, the British master of magnificent horror fiction of a century ago. I've written several well-received essays about Machen for The Friends of Arthur Machen literary society, and one of those essays was just included in the newly published prestigious critical anthology from Hippocampus Press titled Secret Ceremonies. The essay is about one of Machen's final stories, "N".

In addition, the academic publisher McFarland recently released the world's first movie overview book focused entirely on Mars movies, my Mars in the Movies: A History, which discusses 100 films, from the first, being Edison's 5-minute-long A Trip to Mars in 1910 to Ridley Scott's The Martian and beyond.

My e-mail is thomaskentmiller@gmail.com.

The Legend of Robin Hood

In 2014, Airship 27 Productions published Robin Hood – King of Sherwood by I.A. Watson; the first in his trilogy reimagining the saga of fiction's greatest hero. The two sequels, Robin Hood – Arrow of Justice and Robin Hood – Freedom's Outlaw soon followed to the critical delight of fans everywhere.

A few years later, a fourth volume was released containing a collection of Watson's Robin Hood short stories titled, Robin Hood – Forbidden Legends.

Now, at along last, the entire four volumes are offered in this special Omnibus Edition containing all the previous published works. Also included is The Death of Robin Hood, the poignant conclusion to the saga never before in print.

PULP FICTION FOR A NEW GENERATION!

AN AIRSHIP 27 PRODUCTION

AIRSHIP27HANGAR.COM

NEW PULP

the Legend of Robin Hood

I.a. watson